ROAD TO RECOVERY

When her fiancé broke off their engagement, Grace found it hard to carry on as normal, especially with her job in a busy hospital. She even found it hard to accept the help of the new consultant surgeon, Dr Joel Kirkpatrick, who had a reputation of being ruthless in the pursuit of his career and also in his relationships with women. Could she trust him? Could he be the one to mend her broken heart?

*Books by Rachael Croft
in the Linford Romance Library:*

SUMMER'S ILLUSION
WHISPER OF DOUBT
SILENT HEART
A PLACE IN YOUR HEART

RACHAEL CROFT

◆

ROAD TO RECOVERY

Complete and Unabridged

LINFORD
Leicester

First published in Great Britain

First Linford Edition
published 2000

British Library CIP DataCroft

Croft, Rachael
    Road to recovery.—Large print ed.—
Linford romance library
    1. Love stories
    2. Large type books
    I. Title
823.9′14 [F]

ISBN 0–7089–5648–3

Published by
F. A. Thorpe (Publishing) Ltd.
Anstey, Leicestershire

Set by Words & Graphics Ltd.
Anstey, Leicestershire
Printed and bound in Great Britain by
T. J. International Ltd., Padstow, Cornwall

This book is printed on acid-free paper

1

Everything was calm in the Recovery Room at St Margaret's Hospital. Four out of the eight beds were occupied with peacefully sleeping patients returned from theatre. All were stable, there were no emergencies and no more patients expected in for at least half an hour. A couple of nurses were changing a saline drip for one of the patients, their voices hushed, while at the end of the ward, Sister Trainer was briefing her relief prior to the change of shift.

As Grace surveyed the scene she felt a glow of satisfaction. Everything was completed and all necessary charts written up, all were up to date, and there was nothing left for her to do for her two patients before she went off duty. The monitors by each bed sent out their regular signals, but silently.

1

The first thing Grace always did when she came on duty was turn off their irritating bleeps. It was perfectly safe, because if any patient was in trouble an emergency buzzer would sound instantly.

She could see a figure, clad like herself in surgical greens, in the glassfronted office at the end of the ward. It waved and beckoned her in. Presumably it was Ralph, the staff nurse who was to take over from her. Grace wasn't in any rush to go home so she could take time for a chat. Ralph was always a fund of entertaining stories and hospital gossip. And he would need to be warned about that new Ear, Nose and Throat surgeon, the tall rangy one, who seemed to make a point of coming through to see for himself how his patients were being treated. He looked like an awkward customer and had already reduced one of the student nurses to tears.

Still musing, Grace walked into the office and pulled off her green cap, letting her shoulder-length hair cascade round her shoulders. She breathed a sigh of relief.

'That's better! The one downside to this job is having to bundle all my hair up into this thing. Why, Ralph, what's going on?'

She stopped short at the sight of her friend's Cheshire cat grin.

'You look like you've just won the lottery or something. What's the good news?'

She perched on the end of the desk, smiling down at him. Ralph was a good sort, but in the past he'd had problems in his life. She hoped he'd had a bit of good luck for a change, and it looked like she wasn't going to be disappointed.

'Great news, Grace!' Ralph's eyes sparkled. 'It's Maisie. She's pregnant at last! We're going to have a baby, Grace, can you believe it?'

'Oh, Ralph, that's terrific news! This baby couldn't have chosen two nicer parents! When is it expected?'

3

Grace listened with mounting interest as Ralph unfolded the details.

'We'll be having a celebration party next week,' he finished, 'so consider yourself invited. But right now,' he stood up and swept Grace into his arms, 'come waltz with me, my lady.'

'Ralph, you are an idiot!'

But there was no resisting him. Grace allowed herself to be waltzed round the little office. A pile of folders crashed to the ground.

'Don't you think it's a little congested in here?' Grace suggested.

'You're right. Let's try the corridor,' Ralph said laughingly.

He steered her towards a door. Grace bit her lip, trying not to laugh, and hoping that they wouldn't connect with Sister Trainer's ample figure as she returned to her office, but too late. As they went through the door there was a bump, and Grace felt her waist clasped from behind. Something wasn't right. Grace felt as if she was encircled by steel bars.

4

There was a sudden, awful silence. Grace, looking into Ralph's face, saw it flood with embarrassed colour. A ghastly thought struck her. Of all the people to bump into, surely it couldn't be . . .

The hands released her, and slowly, reluctantly she turned to find her worst fears confirmed. The figure that confronted her was clad in anonymous surgical green, but there was no mistaking those angular features, the firm lips thinned into a straight line of disdain. It was St Margaret's newest consultant surgeon, Joel Kirkpatrick.

Grace opened her mouth and closed it again. Never in all her twenty-four years had she felt quite such a fool. Behind her Ralph croaked into speech.

'I'm sorry, sir, it's my fault. Maisie's pregnant, and . . . '

'Spare me the excuses.'

One long-fingered hand waved in dismissal.

'Just get out there and do the job you're paid to do. My patient is back

5

from theatre and there's only a student nurse free. Meanwhile, you two are having your own private party in here. This isn't good enough.'

Grace had to repress an exclamation of surprise. Back already! This man was a fast worker. They'd have to remember that in future. Ralph was already through the door.

'I'll attend to this, Grace. You get off home. I can only repeat that I'm sorry, sir. I can assure you this won't happen again.'

'It had better not.'

The words were a curt throwaway as Joel Kirkpatrick turned on his heel and strode off down the corridor without a backward glance. Ralph hesitated on the threshold, looking back at Grace anxiously. There was a brief, tense silence. Grace broke it first.

'Sorry. I was going to warn you about him.'

Ralph smiled wryly.

'I don't think you need to now. He

doesn't exactly radiate sweetness and light, does he?'

'No way.'

Subdued, Grace followed Ralph back into the recovery room for a last check round before she left. No, it wasn't going to be easy working with Mr High-and-Mighty-Kirkpatrick, but, she consoled herself, at least the next day was Saturday, and her day off, and there would be a letter from Simon.

Simon's letters always arrived on Saturdays. Ever since he'd got that engineering contract in Germany he'd written regularly to Grace and the letters had been something for her to look forward to through the week. He'd never missed. It was so like him, methodical, organised, reliable. People were always telling Grace how lucky she was to be engaged to such a marvel. Ideal husband material, her mother was always saying.

His letters were always so entertaining, full of detail about the people he'd met, how his work was going, his trips around the German countryside. Perhaps of late they'd been a little briefer than usual, but Grace understood how his work was sometimes very demanding. He'd revert to his normal chatty style once things got easier.

This particular Saturday, as she picked up the letters and carried them through into the kitchen, picking out the one from Simon as she went, she wondered if he would make any mention of when he was coming back. His last few letters hadn't said anything about it. In fact, they really had been brief to the point of brusqueness now she thought about it. Her brow creased in a frown. She hoped he wasn't under too much pressure at work.

She sat down at the kitchen table holding the envelope. It felt thin and her spirits dropped a little. Just when she could have done with a nice long, newsy letter to cheer her up, but, she thought, as she slit it open and pulled out the single sheet of notepaper it contained, even if it just tells me when he'll be home for Easter, that'll be enough for me.

The next moment the thin sheet fluttered to the floor unheeded.

Simon was not coming back for Easter. He would never be coming back, at least not to Grace. He'd met a German girl, an accountant, who worked for the same firm. They'd fallen in love. It had happened as a complete surprise. No-one could have expected it. His small, neat handwriting revealed everything, relentlessly. He was terribly sorry.

He realised Grace would be upset, angry even. She would find it hard to forgive him or to understand, but he begged her to try. He was going to spend Easter with the girl's family. In the summer, he would bring her over to Britain and he hoped that she and Grace could meet if Grace was agreeable.

Her fingers clenched into tight, angry fists. How dare this German female come along and steal her fiancé? And as for Simon! Well, now she could see why his letters had been so brief of late. How naïve, how plain stupid of her not to have guessed the reason! Hot tears welled up and started to fall. Grace let them come. There was some comfort in it.

At last she wiped her eyes and got up from the table. She glanced at the clock. It was after nine, she realised with a shock of surprise. Where had the time gone? There were things to be done. OK, she'd just been jilted, but life had to go on. She wasn't the only one in the world suffering heartache. And whatever her emotional state, there was the weekend shopping to be done.

A flurry of rain beat against the window. Grace noticed it without surprise. It was just the weather she'd have chosen for such an occasion — grey and miserable. At least it wasn't a waste of a fine day. Mechanically she got up and found a raincoat, then her shoulder bag and checked that her purse was in it. It was quite a walk to the shops, but she didn't mind. It would give her time to think, time to consider how to fill the chasm Simon Grant had left.

With only the haziest idea of where she was heading, she turned up the collar of her raincoat and went out, hardly noticing which way she was going, relying on autopilot to take her to the shops. Then it seemed that everything happened at once.

A horn blared, tyres screeched. Somewhere behind her a door slammed, a voice shouted something. Still Grace made no connection between these events and herself until suddenly, violently, her arm was seized and she was yanked round to face one very angry man. In fact, she realised, coming out of her trance into horrified awareness, it was one very angry Joel Kirkpatrick. Flint-grey eyes bored into hers, conveying an anger that was almost tangible.

'What on earth do you think you

were doing? Have you a death wish or something?'

Grace ran her tongue over suddenly dry lips. What was the man raving about? Surely it was nothing to do with her, whatever it was. Was he some sort of maniac, or was this some continuation of the events of the previous day? Dazedly she looked around, searching for some sort of clue to his outrageous behaviour, then she saw the road junction, the pedestrian lights firmly on red, the car slewed across the road, partially blocking it. And then she realised what she'd done.

'Oh, heavens, I'd no idea — '

The grip on her arm slackened ever so slightly and she felt a tremor run through the long, strong fingers. With a small sense of surprise, Grace realised that she'd given Joel Kirkpatrick quite a scare, and she began to feel distinctly guilty despite her own shock. She looked up into his face. He was so tall she had to tilt her head. She tried to summon up a suitably apologetic smile.

'Look, I'm terribly sorry. I was miles away!'

'Miles away! I only wish you were! You realise you almost caused a serious accident? I had to swerve right across the road to avoid you.'

He stared down into her face and slowly Grace saw amazed recognition dawn.

'Good grief, it's you again! Don't tell me you're so preoccupied with your condition that you don't know what you're doing?'

Condition? What was he talking about? Grace was confused and upset. She couldn't make head nor tail out of what he was saying. A surge of anger against this man welled up in her. All right, she'd been at fault, but just who did he think he was to lecture her like this in the middle of a crowded shopping street, especially when he didn't know the first thing about the trauma she was going through? She wrenched away from his grasp.

'I congratulate you on your presence

of mind,' she bit out. 'Now may I suggest you move your car before someone scratches its precious paint trying to get past?'

Before he could make any reply she swung round on her heel and walked away, hardly caring where she was going, just desperate to get away. Some doors loomed up in front of her. She pushed them open and walked through. Instantly there was peace. Looking round Grace realised she was in Brannigan's, the most prestigious and expensive of the town's department stores. It was a haven of quiet in a bustling world, just the place to stay and calm down, even though normally she rarely ventured inside except perhaps at sale times when the prices were more within her reach.

There was a display of silk scarves nearby, a kaleidoscope of shimmering colours. Attracted by them, Grace moved over and picked one up, letting the soft, sensuous material glide through her fingers. It was oddly soothing, rather like stroking a cat. The thought came to her that one of these would go beautifully with her new suit, soften its rather severe lines. She glanced at the price tag and pursed her lips. On second thoughts, perhaps not. This wasn't self indulgence so much as sheer lunacy.

She made to put it back, then paused. The soft cerise shade was exactly right, and when you spent most of your working life in an unflattering set of surgical greens, aren't you due a little lunacy from time to time? And, of course, a small pitiless voice reminded her, with your wedding to Simon off, you can afford to spend a little more on yourself. No more need to scrimp and save.

Grace screwed up her eyes, unprepared for the sudden anguish of regret that overwhelmed her. Insistent tears pricked at her eyelids and a huge lump in her throat was threatening to choke her. She realised she was about to make an exhibition of herself in the town's most exclusive shop. She had to get out of there and fast.

Hurriedly, oblivious of everything but the need to escape, she made for the stairs and then the nearest exit. She shoved open the doors and got out into the blissful relief of the cool, outside air. Never mind the traffic fumes or the rain on her face, here was freedom. Or was it? A hand was placed on her shoulder, a voice in her ear.

'Excuse me, madam, would you mind accompanying me back into the store?'

Grace whirled round, her mind reeling. For one crazy moment she thought she was being accosted by Joel Kirkpatrick yet again, but then she saw that her assailant was a thin, grim-looking man of uncertain age, whose sparse frame held a surprising amount of strength as she found when she instinctively tried to pull away.

'Get your hands off me! What's going on?'

But even as she spoke, she realised with sickening clarity exactly what was going on. For there, blazing like a beacon, was the end of the expensive cerise scarf, sticking out of her shoulder bag. Her first thought was what a ghastly colour! How could she ever have thought it would suit her? And how could this stupid man possibly think she wanted to possess it, let alone steal it! No, it was an appalling mistake. She'd been upset, that was all, hadn't thought what she was doing. She tried to explain.

'I didn't realise I'd put it in my bag. Here, take the thing. I don't want it. I'm sorry. It was just a mistake, that's all.'

Oh, heavens, people were staring. The man obviously didn't believe a word she said, his expression changed not one iota.

'I must insist you come with me to the manager's office, madam.'

Wildly, Grace glanced around. Surely there was someone who could help, who could tell this awful man he was wrong about her. But there was no-one, except — oh, no, not here!

She turned her head away, but too late. He'd seen her. Joel Kirkpatrick had seen her, and from his one, long appraising glance, Grace realised that he understood only too well what was going on. The blood drained from her face, and without further attempt at argument she followed the store detective back inside. Whatever happened now, she acknowledged, whether she proved her innocence or not, nothing could take away from the awfulness of that moment.

The man ushered her into a small, bare room that overlooked the street. Looking out of the window, Grace had a clear view of the road junction where she'd nearly ended up under the wheels of Joel Kirkpatrick's sports car. She almost found herself wishing that he hadn't managed to stop, then she'd be waking up in a bed in Casualty rather than being here accused of a crime she hadn't committed.

She brought herself up short. This was no way to think! She would explain everything, quite clearly and calmly, then they'd be bound to understand. It wasn't as if she had a criminal record. This was a genuine mistake, made under stress. She rushed into speech, trying to make the store detective see reason.

'Please, will you only let me explain everything, and I'm sure we can sort this out? You see, I got some very bad news this morning, and I — '

The man held up a weary hand.

'I'm sorry, madam, I'm only acting in accordance with company policy. The manager will be here in a moment and then you'll have the procedure explained to you.'

Procedure! Grace's blood ran cold. She buried her head in her hands, trying to think straight. A moment later, she glanced up as the door opened and a woman came in. Grace judged her to be in her early forties, well-groomed and with an air of confidence. This was evidently the store manager. She took a seat behind the desk and clasped her hands.

'Good afternoon, I'm Helen Brannigan. What seems to be the problem?'

Immediately both Grace and the detective launched into speech. The man won by sheer persistence, and Grace had to sit and listen despairingly as he explained what he'd seen. Grace bit her lip. It sounded so convincing. How could her own story possibly be believed? She waited for the caution, for the news that the police were on their way. But amazingly, she heard the manager's soft authoritative voice saying, 'Thank you, Mr Wilkes, you can leave us now.'

Grace stared at the detective, and found him looking just as amazed as she was as he got up and left the room. She waited to see what would happen next, and her surprise grew as Helen Brannigan actually smiled.

'Now, would you mind furnishing me with your name and address? It's only a matter of routine.'

Grace swallowed hard.

'You mean you haven't called the police? You aren't going to prosecute?'

'No, of course not. I can see that you're under stress. Obviously you made a mistake.'

Grace opened her mouth then closed it again. There was no point in trying to ask questions, demand explanations. Let it suffice that the store manager was satisfied that she hadn't intended to take the scarf. As briefly as possible she replied to the questions that were put to her, declined the offer of a cup of coffee, and left the store a few minutes later with a profound sense of relief.

She gave up the idea of doing any shopping. All she wanted to achieve was to get home without any further disasters. If she had to exist on bread and water for the rest of the weekend, that was a minor problem. The major problem would confront her on

Monday at the hospital, because it was then she would have to encounter Joel Kirkpatrick, who'd seen her being led ignominiously away by the store detective. He wasn't to know things had ended happily. In fact, Grace reflected depressingly, for all she knew the story might already be circulating the corridors of St Margaret's and losing nothing in the telling.

How on earth was she going to face everyone, most of all, Joel Kirkpatrick?

2

'You certainly had a lucky escape,' Ralph stated when Grace told him what had happened at Brannigan's.

They were having a coffee together before starting their shift, in the small staff tea-room. In one corner, the consultant gynaecologist was chatting to his theatre sister, while next to them a group of student nurses gossiped together. Grace stared down into her coffee mug, swirling the liquid around in it. She had to agree.

'Yes, I must say I was astonished when the manager said I could go. Even now I don't know why she did it, although I must have thought it through a hundred times. Unless she happened to be looking out of the window when I nearly got mown down by our Mr Kirkpatrick.'

'Hm, could be,' Ralph conceded. 'If

so, he'd be surprised to discover he'd done you a favour by nearly flattening you.'

Grace said nothing. She hadn't told Ralph that Joel Kirkpatrick had seen her being apprehended. She didn't like to dwell on that awful moment herself, even though everything had ended happily. Suddenly she was conscious of a change in the atmosphere. The giggling students were quiet. Even the sonorous tones of the gynaecologist were momentarily stilled. Grace's stomach lurched. Even without turning her head she knew who had just walked in. She didn't need to see Ralph's gaze fixed on her in concern. Footsteps approached over the tiled floor; she heard her name spoken.

'Nurse Bennet?'

She bit her lip, summoning up every reserve of self-control, so that she could turn quite unconcernedly and look up at the man whose long dark shadow enveloped her.

'Yes, Mr Kirkpatrick?'

'I wanted to speak to you.'

Unbidden he lowered himself into the empty seat at her side, ignoring Ralph's indrawn breath of protest.

'You have a few moments?'

It was a statement not a request. Grace glanced across at Ralph.

'Would you excuse us a moment, Ralph? This won't take long.'

She raised her eyebrows fractionally, to indicate to him that she was quite sure of herself, and Ralph, after only a moment's hesitation, rose and left them, with a brief nod for Joel Kirkpatrick. Silence yawned.

'You wanted to tell me something about your patients this afternoon, Mr Kirkpatrick?' she prompted.

She slanted him a swift sideways glance as she spoke. He really was a very disconcerting man, the way he leaned back in his chair watching her from under those heavy brows. His cool, appraising stare was frighteningly perceptive. It made her feel almost as if he could see right into her mind.

'Let's cut the pussyfooting around, shall we?' he said softly. 'You know why I want to talk to you. I want to know if you're all right.'

Unpleasant images arose in Grace's mind, images she'd rather shut out and forget, and with them a tinge of anger. What right did this man think he had to cross-question her like this? Who asked him to poke his nose into her life? Coolly she returned his stare.

'I thank you for your concern, Mr Kirkpatrick,' she informed him. 'I can assure you that I'm perfectly all right. If I wasn't I wouldn't be here, and as far as I'm concerned, what happened on Saturday is over and done with. I'd be grateful if you wouldn't. mention it again.'

She was gripping the edge of the table as she spoke, and with a twinge of alarm she realised that his candid gaze was fixed on her left hand. More specifically, he was observing the pale band of skin where her engagement ring had used to fit. Immediately she moved her hands, but she knew it was too late. His gaze travelled to her face.

'It's not all right though, is it?' he said bluntly.

Grace felt her face pale. She stood up so abruptly that for a few seconds she felt the floor almost slip away beneath her. Cold anger flooded over her. She hadn't shared the news of her broken engagement with Ralph or anyone yet, and Ralph, despite his genuine friendship and concern for her, hadn't noticed the lack of a ring on her left hand. It had taken the keenness of Joel Kirkpatrick's observation to make the connection.

It didn't seem right that he, a stranger, and a hostile stranger at that, should notice such an intimate detail of her life. She resented it as an intrusion. Suddenly the small tea-room seemed claustrophobic, threatening.

'You must excuse me, Mr Kirkpatrick. It's time I got changed to go on duty.'

Her voice was thick, and she knew he

must find that a lame excuse, but really she couldn't come up with anything better. Without waiting for him to reply, she walked past him and out of the room. She didn't look back, but somehow she knew he was watching her. More than that, she was depressingly aware that because of the events of the weekend she'd managed to arouse his interest. For better or worse, it seemed that she intrigued him.

She gritted her teeth. He probably felt that she was a walking disaster, hardly capable of looking after herself. Would he therefore deduce that she was incapable of doing her job? Oh, no, she thought, I only hope he doesn't put in a complaint. He has no grounds. Let's make sure it stays that way.

'Grace! Grace!'

She turned as she felt her arm being gently tugged, and found Sister Trainer gazing anxiously at her.

'Oh, sorry, Sister, I was miles away. Did you want me?'

'Yes, I did. Nothing urgent. I just

want you to take one of the students in hand for the afternoon. Let her check in a few patients and see them out at the other end. She's a bit scatty, this one, but I know you've plenty of patience. But, Grace, to be frank, you don't quite look yourself today. Is everything all right?'

'I'm fine, honestly. Just had a hectic weekend, that's all.'

Sister Trainer looked relieved.

'Well, as long as it's just that. Not been up to anything that Simon would disapprove of, I hope.'

Grace mumbled something as she sped off down the corridor to the locker room. Well, she'd have to be prepared for that sort of comment, until she felt ready to announce the news of her broken engagement. But strangely enough it didn't hurt quite as much as she'd thought it would. Was she a much stronger person than she'd thought, or was there some other reason?

She was still thinking it over later

when she arrived at the barrier, where patients from the wards were brought down to be checked in for their operations. The student was already there, a thin girl in a set of oversized greens, with stray wisps of mousy hair escaping from under her cap.

'Nurse Bennet?' she enquired anxiously.

'Call me Grace. And you are? Haven't you got a name badge?'

'Oh, I forgot.'

The girl clapped a hand to her mouth.

'I must have left it in the locker room.'

Grace shook her head in mock despair.

'Well, it's not much use there, is it? The lockers don't need to know your name but the patients do. You've got time to get it before the first patient arrives. What's your name by the way?'

'Anita.'

'OK, Anita, I'll see you back in a minute then.'

As Anita dashed off, Grace checked the afternoon list. The next patient was having a small nose operation, and his surgeon was to be Joel Kirkpatrick. Here we go, she thought to herself wearily, but it was a very minor procedure. Anita would be well able to cope with it. She could probably manage to keep right out of the way herself, so there'd be no danger of bumping into the ENT surgeon.

But then Grace closed her eyes momentarily as something occurred to her. This student, Anita, was the girl who'd been reduced to tears by Joel Kirkpatrick the previous Friday. It looked as though she'd better be on hand after all to ensure that everything was carried out properly and Mr Kirkpatrick had no cause for complaint.

Anita scurried back, complete with name badge, just as the bed containing the patient, Mr Templeton, was wheeled down from the ward by a porter. A ward nurse walked alongside.

'Let's see you do this, Anita,' Grace

prompted. 'You know the questions to ask. Keep it easy and informal.'

At Anita's nod, she went forward with her to greet the patient, an elderly man with a worried expression, only slightly dopey from his medication.

'Good afternoon, Mr Templeton. My name's Grace and this is Anita who's going to check you in for your operation. She'll have a few questions to ask you. I dare say you've heard them all before.'

She smiled encouragingly at Anita who stepped forward to begin the checks. Meanwhile Grace had a word with the ward nurse who rolled her eyes at the sight of the girl.

'So you've got dear Anita. I wish you joy of her.'

'Why? She doesn't seem that bad.'

'Maybe not now, but if there's any sort of crisis, she tends to lose her head. And that Mr Templeton's a heavy smoker by the way. The anaesthetist was making warning noises about him. It was very borderline as to whether he'd get his operation at all today.'

'OK, we'll bear that in mind.'

Grace watched as the elderly man, supported by Anita and the porter, slowly transferred from his bed to the trolley. The ward nurse moved forward to make up the bed which would be taken to the exit room ready to receive the patient after his operation. Grace noted approvingly that Anita had remembered to ask the porter to remove the bedhead. That would be taken separately to the recovery room. If the patient needed resuscitation it could be carried out more easily without the bedhead being on.

'Right,' she said to the porter, 'this patient's ready as soon as they call for him. We'll see you later, Mr Templeton. You're going to be taken through to the anaesthetic room now, and I'm afraid they'll ask you these questions all over again. But you'll soon be back with us. It will probably only seem like five minutes or so. Anita here will stay with you until you go through.'

A voice on the intercom told her that the next patient was ready to be checked in, a gastric patient who would be going into Intensive Care after the operation. Grace felt herself relax immediately. Frank Foster, the consultant in charge, was an easy-going character. There'd be no problems there. If only all consultants were the same!

An hour later, Mr Templeton was wheeled out of theatre by the anaesthetist, who was a young, recently qualified female doctor, and a porter. Grace beckoned Anita forward.

'Here we go. You show me what you do now.'

She stood back to let the student take charge, all too conscious of a prickle of tension. Silly really, everything was bound to be straightforward after such a simple procedure, but she knew that soon Joel Kirkpatrick would be sweeping through the double doors to see his patient. It was vitally important that he should find everything to his liking.

Anita twisted a corner of her skirt, a worrying sign, Grace noted. Was she, too, on edge about Joel Kirkpatrick?

'Is there anything we need to know about this patient?' Anita asked the anaesthetist diffidently.

'We've got him on oxygen,' the anaesthetist replied. 'His breathing isn't too good. You know he's a smoker, so we'll need to keep an eye on that. I'll be in the tea-room if you want me. I'm desperate for a cuppa, but I have my pager.'

Without waiting for an answer, she left along with the porter.

Grace raised her eyebrows slightly. In theory, the anaesthetist should stay with her patient if there was likely to be any cause for alarm. Anita should have insisted on that. She almost stepped forward and intervened, but decided against it.

She didn't want to sap the girl's confidence by going over her head. Besides, it would be easy enough to contact the anaesthetist if necessary.

She turned to Anita.

'Right, what do we do first?'

Anita checked off on her fingers.

'Check the airway, attach him to the walled oxygen, and the blood pressure monitor and the pulsometer.'

'And the oxygen is set at?'

'Four litres per minute?' Anita hazarded.

'Right. That's the normal setting, we'll see how he does on that. You get on and do it, I'll write it up.'

She observed Anita's progress as she wrote the notes up herself. Everything was done satisfactorily.

'Now what?' she asked when Anita had finished.

'Well, we'd examine the wound, but we can't do that because he has a nasal pack in, and he hasn't got a drip in, so I suppose we can just leave him to it for a bit.'

'Well, yes, up to a point. Remember what the anaesthetist said. We must keep an eye on his breathing. Meanwhile, Mrs Travers here is ready to have her drip changed.'

'Right.'

Anita hurried off, leaving Grace momentarily free. It was nice to have a breathing space and normally she might have wandered over to have a chat with one of the other staff nurses, but this morning she couldn't relax. It was the knowledge that at any moment Joel Kirkpatrick would be casting his critical eye over her work.

'Grace!' Anita was calling. 'Mrs Travers is regaining consciousness. Can I get her to spit out the airway yet?'

'Let me look,' Grace said as she went over. 'You mustn't do that too soon or she might choke on her tongue. Mrs Travers? Are you awake?'

The woman's eyelids fluttered, but didn't open.

'I'd wait a bit yet until you're sure she's come round. Don't forget her chart must be written up every fifteen minutes. OK?'

'OK. It should be due in about — oh, what's that?'

Grace was already moving. The insistent note of the alarm worked on her instantly. Everything was instinctive. She hurried round from Mrs Travers's bedside to Mr Templeton, noting at once the sudden dramatic fall in his blood pressure. Over her shoulder she threw a command to Anita as another nurse hurried over to assist.

'Get that anaesthetist back, right now!'

The right procedure was second nature, and she quickly carried out all the necessary steps. Oh, please, she prayed silently, please don't let Joel Kirkpatrick come in now. But it was too late. As she eventually straightened up and look round, she found herself the subject of no less than four pairs of eyes. Sister Trainer was hurrying down the centre of the ward, the guilty looking anaesthetist who still had a digestive biscuit in her hand, a wide-eyed stare from a very flustered Anita, and worst of all, Joel Kirkpatrick. Grace groaned inwardly. Was this man destined always to be on hand at her worst moments? He stood back a little from the rest, but there was a dangerous glint in his eyes as he watched the efficient performance of the emergency procedures.

He waited until everything was done, until the patient was stabilised, the anaesthetist had carried out her checks, very thoroughly, and pronounced herself satisfied. Sister Trainer had taken a red-faced Anita away for a motherly chat in her office. It didn't seem fair, Grace thought numbly. She was the only one left to face the wrath to come. When it came it was ominously quiet.

'Can I have a word, nurse?'

He was already moving out into the corridor. Aware of the sympathetic looks of the other staff nurses, Grace followed him. Once outside he turned and looked down at her, his brown-eyed gaze like two points of light.

'You nearly lost my patient.'

'Emergencies happen,' she said, speaking slowly because she felt that if she didn't she would end up babbling and incoherent. 'He seemed to be fine. It all happened so suddenly.'

'Emergencies happen because people aren't prepared for them.'

Grace could see that Joel was tense and tight-lipped, as if he had to try very hard not to lose his temper with her.

'Surely the anaesthetist explained that there was a danger with this patient. He was known to be a heavy smoker.'

'Yes, but — '

Grace tailed off. She couldn't bring herself to put blame on the anaesthetist, or on Anita, and anyway, she reminded herself bitterly, the ultimate responsibility was her own. Once again Joel threw her own words back at her.

'Yes, but isn't good enough, Grace, and you know it. Patients shouldn't be at risk after routine operations. And don't think I'm unaware of the anaesthetist's part in all this. I intend to tell her exactly what I think about it. But you shouldn't have let her slope off. You were in charge of the patient.'

Grace opened her mouth to begin an explanation, then closed it again. Any attempt at self-justification would throw all the blame on Anita.

'I'm sorry,' she managed, forcing herself to meet that bleak gaze. 'I'll make sure it doesn't happen again.'

Her apology was greeted with a sigh.

'That's not good enough, Grace, and you know it. Look, I was told that you were one of the best nurses in this department, clearly destined for higher things. At least that's what your superiors think. What do I find? First, a woman who prefers to dance while the patients look after themselves. Second, a zombie who nearly throws herself under the wheels of my car. Third . . .'

'All right!' Grace almost shouted at him, definitely not wanting to hear any more. 'So you caught me at a bad moment.'

'Several bad moments. Do you make a habit of them?'

Grace said nothing, so he went on.

'You're not performing well, Grace

Bennet, and it's time something was done about it. On present evidence you don't seem capable of doing anything to sort your life out, so I intend to step in. To start with, I'm going to pick you up at the end of your shift and take you out for a meal. You look as if you could use one.'

Grace stared at him, her simmering resentment flaring to red-hot anger. She could hardly believe what she was hearing. This man was calmly announcing that she wasn't capable of running her own life and that he intended to do it for her. Was that it? She felt like slapping him across the face, but somehow she retained enough consciousness of hospital etiquette to realise that you didn't do that to a consultant surgeon. Instead, she forced herself to take a slow, calming breath and say perfectly politely, 'Thank you, Mr Kirkpatrick, but I think I can manage my own life unaided.'

He was unfazed.

'In that case, come for a meal

anyhow. I don't suppose you have anything else planned.'

His calm assurance was absolutely infuriating. Grace had difficulty in restraining the impulse to scream at him. Unfortunately in her heated state she didn't quite have the presence of mind to invent some convincing prior engagement, and could only manage, 'No, I don't, but — '

'Then let's consider it settled. You finish at five today, don't you? I'll pick you up at the carpark entrance at five past.'

'Mr Kirkpatrick, I — '

'Nurse Bennet!'

Sister Trainer had appeared at the doorway.

'We've three patients arrived back. Could you give us a hand here, please?'

Grace had no choice but to go. The ward sister was waiting for her, so she had no chance of telling Joel Kirkpatrick exactly what she thought of his kind invitation. She had to content herself with a stilted, 'I'm sorry, sir, that is not at all convenient,' as she left him.

Sister Trainer started to tell her about the patient who was allotted to her, but Grace found it hard to concentrate. She was forcefully aware that Joel Kirkpatrick seemed to have decided to interfere in her life. And although she might have succeeded in fobbing him off this time, she wasn't going to be able to keep him at bay for ever.

3

At the end of her shift Grace tossed her surgical greens into the laundry basket with a less good aim than usual. They landed at Ralph's feet just as he was coming out of the men's locker room.

'What's this?'

He picked them up with a grin and dropped them into the basket.

'Trying to trip me up, were you? What have I done to deserve such treatment?'

'Sorry, Ralph.' Grace smiled ruefully. 'I suppose I'm a bit preoccupied.'

Ralph fell into step beside her as they walked up the long corridor towards the exit.

'I can guess why. I heard about your little experience with our surgeon friend this afternoon. If it's any consolation, he certainly told that anaesthetist what he thought of her. I crashed in on them

45

in the tea-room and just as quickly crashed out again.'

Grace sighed.

'It's not that. I didn't want to get anyone into trouble, and anyway it was my fault really. I should have insisted she stayed.'

'Well, everything ended up all right anyhow,' Ralph soothed. 'Mr Templeton is back on his ward, completely unaware of all the fuss, and little Anita has had a good lesson that she won't forget in a hurry. As for Joel Kirkpatrick, well he's bound to have other things to think about. It will all blow over, you wait and see.'

'I hope so.'

Grace tried to sound more confident than she felt. Already she was inclined to doubt whether her put-off of Joel had been sufficiently forceful. She hadn't seen anything of him since the invitation as he'd been busy all day. At the end of the corridor she said goodbye to Ralph and started off for the bus stop by the hospital gates, turning up her collar against the rain, but she had scarcely gone ten yards when a voice hailed.

'Grace! Over here!'

She turned to see Joel Kirkpatrick, at the wheel of his car, waving at her.

'Mr Kirkpatrick! What is it? What do you want?'

'I'm here to give you a lift home. This is no weather to be hanging around at bus stops.'

Grace fixed him with a stony stare.

'That's very kind of you, but I can manage.'

'Grace, I'm going to stay here until you get in this car. What are you afraid of, for heaven's sake? It's not as if I'm some sinister stranger.'

Grace turned to see a queue of cars already building up, and not too happy about it either. The longer this went on, she realised with a sinking heart, the more she'd be provoking gossip about herself and Joel Kirkpatrick. Bowing to the inevitable, she got into the car, resolved to say as little as possible on the journey, then thank him politely and get out.

The journey back to Grace's small, terraced cottage was swift and smooth. Definitely superior to the bus, she had to admit to herself as she reclined in the soft leather seat while Joel guided the car skilfully through the rush hour traffic. She was relieved that he didn't make any controversial remarks during the trip. He seemed to prefer to concentrate on his driving, leaving her to listen to some soothing classical music.

She was beginning to enjoy the sensation by the time they pulled up outside the neat row of nineteenth century dwellings where she lived.

'Very nice,' he commented as he stopped the car. 'Much superior to these anonymous flats you get on the edge of town. I'd no idea this little row of houses was tucked away down here.'

'Yes, that's what everyone says.'

Grace was pleased at his approval. Her parents had protested when she'd decided to buy the cottage, and had tried to persuade her to go for something more modern, but she'd stuck out for what she wanted.

'There used to be a cotton mill somewhere here and these were the workers' houses. They are very pretty, but in fairness they do have their drawbacks. No fitted kitchens or central heating, though I'm lucky, mine has got storage radiators.'

'But the character of the place more than makes up for a bit of inconvenience,' Joel said looking around at the neat front gardens.

'It certainly does, and as for the inconvenience, well, that can be changed. We're going to put in a fitted kitchen when — '

She stopped, biting her lip. Foolishly she was forgetting how her life had changed. That fitted kitchen would never go in now, without Simon's do-it-yourself skills. She glanced up, and found a pair of eyes watching her thoughtfully. A large white handkerchief was thrust into her hands.

'Here, blow your nose and let's go inside. It helps to talk.'

Grace began to protest, but Joel was already out of the car and walking round to open the door for her with old-fashioned courtesy. It was now raining quite hard, and he had got an umbrella out of the boot. It made sense to accept its shelter as far as the front porch, but once there Grace summoned up her reserves of determination and turned to him. She tried to speak with as much conviction as possible.

'Look, thank you for the lift, it was very kind of you. But I really don't need sorting out or whatever you choose to call it. I'm a big girl now and I can run my own life.'

Out of the corner of her eye she could see her next-door neighbour returning from the shops, and that gave fresh impetus to her desire to escape indoors. Mrs Roberts was a great observer of other people's business, and Grace knew that the sight of a strange, good-looking man on the doorstep would be bound to set off a round of ever-so-casual questions. She took out her door key and inserted it into the lock. Annoyingly it stuck. Grace began to get ruffled. That had been one of the job's she'd been leaving for Simon. Now it looked as though she'd have to get busy with a screwdriver herself.

'Here, let me.'

Strong, capable hands gently removed the key from her grasp and began to twist it in the lock. Grace stood back, almost dancing with impatience.

'I'm sorry, it's often like that. You just have to get it a certain way.'

Joel glanced briefly at her over his shoulder.

'And now the boyfriend's no longer around you have to deal with these things yourself. He's really left you in the lurch, hasn't he?'

'What do you mean?' Grace snapped.

The lock clicked open, but neither of them took any notice. They just stood

51

facing each other on the threshold.

'All right, if you want me to spell it out for you, I simply mean that you're on your own, and you're pregnant!'

There was a sudden crash as Mrs Roberts' shopping cascaded all over her garden path. Grace threw her a frantic sideways glance and found her open-mouthed, her amazed expression a mirror of Grace's own. Then she stared up at Joel, her mouth working soundlessly.

'Well,' he inquired with deliberate casualness, 'are you going to stand there like a stranded fish, or are you going to invite me in?'

Somehow Grace resisted the impulse to scream incoherently at the top of her lungs. Completely ignoring Mrs Roberts, she pushed at the door and almost fell inside as it opened abruptly. Once in the house, she slammed the door and leaned against it, breathing heavily. To her annoyance, Joel had managed to get inside, too, and he stood facing her in the narrow hallway. Tension stretched between them, taut as a wire.

'All right, calm down,' Joel said quietly. 'I'm sorry if your neighbour's just got an earful of what doesn't concern her, but she'd find out soon enough anyway. Suppose I go and put the kettle on. Which way's the kitchen?'

When Grace made no reply, he pushed open a door at random, and, as luck would have it, turned out to be right first time. He walked inside, ducking his head under the low doorway, and stood looking around him.

'This is nice. I wouldn't spoil it with fitted units. It has character. Now where's the kettle?'

Grace felt that some action was required. She followed him into the kitchen.

'Look, forget the kettle,' she got out through taut lips. 'Just do me the courtesy of explaining that last remark.'

Joel turned to face her, leaning against the pine table in the centre of the room. He thought for a moment.

'I said I wouldn't spoil this kitchen with fitted units.'

'No, not that!' Grace was on a knife edge of tension. 'You said I was pregnant!' she almost spat out.

'Well, yes. You surely haven't forgotten our first meeting when I found you dancing round the hospital with your friend, Ralph, to celebrate that fact? I can only presume your boyfriend wasn't as happy with the idea and that's why he left.'

'Oh, for heaven's sake! It wasn't me!' She saw his eyebrows meet in a puzzled frown and rushed on.

'What I mean is, it's not me who's pregnant. It's Maisie, Ralph's wife. You must have misheard.'

Joel stood still for a moment, clearly coming to terms with this news. Then, abruptly, he began to laugh, filling the house with the noise. Grace stared at him furiously.

'What's so funny?'

'Only the look on your neighbour's

face. I bet she's on the phone right now telling all her friends. We've really set the cat amongst the pigeons.'

Grace turned her back on him and stared out into the garden.

'I don't think it's at all amusing,' she said stiffly. 'You forget that I actually have to live here, and I can tell you I don't enjoy being the subject of the neighbours' little-tattle.'

The laughter died down.

'I'm sorry, Grace. I take your point. What can I do to help? I could go and tell her I made a mistake.'

'Oh, forget it!' Grace sighed wearily. 'That would only make things worse.'

Suddenly she felt the need for a good strong cup of tea. Her legs were threatening to give way. She reached for the kettle and filled it.

'You might as well stay and have a cuppa. If they're going to gossip, let's give them something to gossip about.'

She sat down at the table, and completely against her will a reluctant smile tugged at the corner of her mouth as she remembered Mrs Roberts' gobsmacked expression.

'Oh, it was rather funny, wasn't it? Poor woman, I wonder if I ought to go out and help her pick everything up.'

'She'll have done it by now. And anyway, don't we want her to think that we're upstairs, indulging in illicit passion?'

Grace couldn't help laughing. It was good to laugh again when just forty-eight hours previously, she'd sat in this very kitchen crying her eyes out.

The kettle whistled, she got up and began to make the tea, defiantly shutting out those disturbing images. She opened a packet of shortbread, put it on the table along with the tea things, and sat down opposite Joel. Her eyes caught his and skittered away, nervously. Both of them seemed aware of the change in atmosphere. Joel was first to break the silence.

'There's one thing I'm not wrong about, Grace. He's gone, whoever he is. Why don't you tell me about it?'

Grace waved a dismissive hand.

'I don't want to talk about it. I haven't talked to anyone.'

'Not even Ralph? Or your parents?'

'No. I'm not ready.'

Joel took a sip of tea, his candid gaze probing her face. At last he said, 'You must love him very much.'

The response was an automatic, 'Yes.'

'Why not talk about it? It's often easier to share things with a stranger. If not a stranger, then a mere colleague. I'm more concerned about your job, Grace. I don't really want to pry into your personal life.'

Grace felt her body stiffen. Her instinctive reaction was to refuse, but something prevented her. Perhaps it would be therapeutic to share her experience with this frighteningly perceptive man. As he said, he was a stranger, motivated only by a desire to help. She was sure she could rely on his discretion. She exhaled a long, slow breath.

'All right,' she said slowly. 'I'll tell

you all about Simon.'

It didn't take long. In fact, Grace was surprised how little there was to say about a relationship that had lasted over two years. As she spoke, she dimly began to realise that for a long time now she and Simon had been taking each other for granted, especially during his time in Germany when all she'd had were his letters. Simon as a person was almost as much a stranger as this tall, lean man sitting opposite her, his long fingers cupped round his mug as he listened.

'And then on Saturday morning I got his last letter,' she went on steadily. 'It was a Dear John letter, or in this case, Dear Jane, telling me that he'd met this girl in Germany and fallen in love with her. He was very good about it. He was obviously trying to tell me as gently as he could, but all the same it was an awful shock, and that's why I nearly walked under your car.'

Joel nodded.

'Once I calmed down I realised you

couldn't have been quite yourself. And I suppose that's when I put two and two together and jumped to the wrong conclusion.'

Grace stared down at the table top. Little beads of spilled tea winked at her from its smooth, scrubbed surface. Already her memory had run on, to that cringe-making moment when the detective had apprehended her outside Brannigan's. That must rank as one of the lowest points of my life, she thought numbly. But she had to go on and speak about it. Maybe getting it out into the open would exorcise the sense of shame. She took a deep breath.

'And then I walked into Brannigan's.'

Joel sat quietly and let her tell the story, his shuttered features giving no hint of his reaction. At last Grace got to the end, her relief self-evident.

'Even now I don't know why they let me off so easily,' she confessed. 'You hear those awful stories about people being prosecuted and fined, when I'm sure the whole thing was just some awful mistake. But how do you make the authorities understand? I had absolutely no way of proving that I hadn't intended to take that scarf? Why did Helen Brannigan just allow me to go?'

'I think I can explain that.'

Joel's words fell into the quietness like pebbles into a still pool. When Grace looked up in surprise, he went on.

'I saw what was happening, and when they took you inside, I followed. I managed to get to Ms Brannigan before she saw you. I explained that you had just had a very narrow escape. I came the 'I am a doctor' bit. It can be quite useful at times! I told her that you were probably in a state of shock and not really aware of what you were doing. I'm pleased to find that my efforts on your behalf were so effective.'

Grace flushed. So she owed her freedom, her good name, perhaps even her job, to this man! Well, that put her in his debt and no mistake. Then a sudden awful thought flashed across her mind.

'You didn't say that I was — '

'Pregnant?' Joel finished for her. 'No, I didn't. Credit me with a little discretion, even though you wouldn't think it from that little episode with your neighbour. And now, how about that meal?'

'Meal?' Grace echoed, not realising for a moment what he was talking about.

'I was going to take you out, remember? You look as if you haven't had a square meal in ages.'

It was true enough. Ever since Saturday Grace had had no appetite. On her own at home with nothing to think about but her own disappointed hopes she hadn't felt like cooking anything. Her first impulse was to accept gladly, but then she reconsidered.

'That's very kind of you, but I'd rather not go out for a meal just now.

I've got something ready prepared and I don't want it to go to waste. And to tell you the truth I'm not in the mood for eating out. Another time perhaps?'

It was a lame excuse and she knew it. She waited for Joel to sweep her feeble excuses aside and insist that she accompanied him, but amazingly he made no attempt to persuade her. Instead he got up with a slight shrug of his broad shoulders.

'OK, fair enough. I don't want to railroad you into anything, but don't think you can get rid of me that easily. I intend to keep an eye on you for a while, Grace Bennet. Someone needs to. Don't come to the door, I'll let myself out. I'll give your neighbour a special wave.'

And with that he turned and left, leaving Grace feeling slightly dazed. She wondered just what she'd let herself in for. She hardly knew Joel Kirkpatrick. All right, he'd provided a sympathetic ear, but hadn't he said quite plainly that he was interested in her not so much as a person but as a skilled nurse. If he wanted to help her it was because he wanted to make sure she was up to her job.

She knew enough of her own feelings to be aware that she was in a highly vulnerable state, and she'd seen too many of her friends hurt by on-the-rebound romances to wish to do the same herself. She recalled the vision of Joel Kirkpatrick's handsome profile, and the lurch in the pit of her stomach told her all she needed to know. She was in grave danger of getting emotionally entangled with this man, and that wouldn't do at all.

4

Grace saw nothing of Joel Kirkpatrick the following day, but her acceptance of a lift from him had not gone unnoticed. True to form, hospital gossip had picked up on it and several people made certain they mentioned it to her with varying degrees of interest. Even Anita had heard the news.

'Is it true, Grace? Mr Kirkpatrick gave you a lift home?'

'Yes, he did.'

Grace had to make a big effort not to be short with the girl. She tried to change the subject.

'Look, this patient has had major surgery. We have to observe him carefully. Do you know what we look for following his type of operation?'

Anita checked off on her fingers all the signs she'd be on the look-out for.

'What's he like? I mean, really like?'

she said as she finished.

'Who? The patient?' Grace queried.

'No, silly, Mr Kirkpatrick. I mean, what did you find to talk about? I'd just have died if I was alone with him. I wouldn't know what to say.'

Grace pursed her lips. She had virtually told him all her life story, she thought ruefully. Not for the first time she regretted being quite so free and easy with the details of her personal life. Why, she'd given Joel Kirkpatrick quite a hold over her if he chose to take it. He really caught me at a weak moment, she accused herself.

Fortunately, Anita had no chance to make any further enquiries as to Grace's relationship with the great man as they were kept pretty busy after that. It was a particularly rushed day with quite a high number of emergencies adding to the workload.

By the time she finished her shift, she was worn out, physically and mentally, but as she walked to the bus stop down the road from the hospital the late afternoon sunshine and the bright freshness of the outside air acted on her like a tonic. Despite her tired feet she decided to walk on farther than her usual bus stop and enjoy the summer weather after being inside all day. She could always do a bit of window shopping as she went along.

Suddenly she paused, a stab of unwelcome memory running through her. She was standing outside Brannigan's just where she'd been hauled back in by the store detective, and that was the junction where she'd nearly landed under the wheels of Joel Kirkpatrick's car. She felt her cheeks redden in embarrassment at the recollection, and her overriding impulse was to hurry on by.

But then she stopped. She couldn't run away for ever. Deliberately she paused, took a deep breath then pushed open the heavy plate glass doors of Brannigan's and walked inside.

An hour later, a new dress was hanging in her wardrobe. Grace still could hardly believe what she'd done. It was complete madness. For a start, when would she have an occasion to wear a designer dress? But she didn't care. The purchase had meant something far more than that. It had asserted her independence and shown her that she'd come to terms with the Brannigan's incident.

Now she could draw a line under all that and face the future with confidence, and just at that moment the future meant being able to collapse into bed, with the comforting knowledge that she was on late shift the following day and so she could enjoy a blissful lie-in. It was only as she drifted off to sleep that she realised with a little stab of surprise that she hadn't thought about Simon all day.

Grace yawned and turned over, burrowing deeply into the softness of her pillow. She opened one eye and checked the clock by the side of her bed. It was only nine-thirty. No need to get up for ages yet. So what had woken her? The sound came again, a regular, insistent knocking on the front door.

'Oh, go away!' she muttered crossly, hauling the duvet round her ears to block out the sound.

But the knocking continued. Whoever it was quite clearly wasn't going to give up and go away. She was going to have to get up, and at least, she consoled herself as she pushed back the blankets, she'd managed to last until half past nine. The knocking came again as she threw on her housecoat and ran downstairs. She was sure now it must be some medical emergency and steeled herself for the sight of some distraught, elderly neighbour on the doorstep. But instead when she hauled open the door her anxious gaze fell on the tall, lean form of Joel Kirkpatrick.

'You! What on earth are you doing here? You woke me up, do you realise?'

Joel smiled down at her.

'Sorry. I guess I hadn't got you down

as the sort of person to lounge around in bed on your days off. I thought you were the active type.'

Grace smiled thinly.

'Well, thank you for that instant analysis of my character. As you can see, you got it quite wrong. Might I ask why you found it necessary to come visiting? Surely not just to test your theory as to what time I get up? Or is this your latest idea for scandalising my neighbours?'

The dark eyes twinkled in amusement.

'My, we have got out of the wrong side of the bed, haven't we? Suppose we continue this conversation inside, else we'll have all the lace curtains twitching for miles around.'

Grace gave a frantic glance up and down the street. It wouldn't have surprised her if Mrs Roberts had suddenly popped up from behind the hedge, weeding trowel in hand, but mercifully there was no-one in sight. All the same there was something to be said for conducting this conversation inside. It couldn't take long, surely.

'All right,' she said reluctantly, 'you'd better come in.'

Inside the hall, she turned to face him, making no move to enter the kitchen or the small sitting-room. Whatever he had to say, she decided, he could say it here and get it over with.

'So, to what do I owe the pleasure of your company this time, Mr Kirkpatrick?'

The dark eyes held hers.

'Joel, remember?'

He held up something, and Grace recognised it as a toolbox, but her mind still refused to make any connection. She stared at him blankly.

'Sorry?'

'You really aren't at your best first thing in the morning, are you, Grace? How about putting the kettle on for a good strong cup of coffee and meanwhile I can get on with what I came to do, namely, mend the lock on your front door.'

'Oh!'

Grace was dumbfounded. Suddenly she felt a complete heel. The man had turned up purely out of goodwill to do her a favour, and here she was treating him like something that had crawled out from under a stone. She was filled with repentance and a desire to make it up to him. A cup of coffee was the least she could do.

'That's so kind of you,' she said thankfully. 'I'd forgotten about the lock. I suppose it didn't occur to me that you'd be good at that sort of thing.'

'There's a lot we don't know about each other, eh, Grace?'

His tone had changed, darkened somehow, and Grace felt suddenly uncomfortable under his steady gaze.

'Will it take long?' she asked.

'No, only a few minutes. It's an easy job, so you don't need to be too impressed.'

'Right. I'll bring you a coffee.'

She made one and took it through to the hall where Joel was unscrewing the

71

broken lock. Her gaze moved to his fingers, long and sensitive, surgeon's fingers. Now they were deftly working on the lock, just as surely as they must work on any of his patients. Quickly she went upstairs and put on a pair of jeans and a loosely belted top. It felt strange getting dressed in her room with Joel in the house downstairs. She smiled to herself, visualising Anita's amazement if she could see them now. She fastened her hair back and went downstairs. To her surprise Joel had just about finished.

'There, I told you it was straightforward. All I had to do was take the old one out and put the new one in. A bit like transplant surgery, actually.'

His eyes ran over Grace in frank appreciation.

'You should wear jeans more often. You've got just the figure for them.'

'I wear them a lot at home,' Grace responded. 'Just because you always see me in surgical greens doesn't mean I happen to like shapeless, ill-fitting clothes.'

'Touché.'

He grinned at her, and Grace felt herself smiling back before she retreated into the kitchen. How deceptive first impressions could be, she thought, as she tidied things away and wiped over the worktops. At her first meeting with Joel she'd put him down as insensitive and generally arrogant, and she knew that was how he was seen by many of her colleagues.

Yet here she was seeing quite another side to him, genuinely concerned for her and doing his best to help. She felt a glowing warmth slowly start to build somewhere inside her. She was seeing another side of Joel Kirkpatrick and she liked what she saw, very much. And the fact that he chose to reveal this side of his character to so very few people made it all the more intriguing.

A few minutes later he came into the

kitchen and dumped his toolbox on the floor.

'That's it, finished,' he announced. 'You shouldn't have any more trouble with your lock now.'

Grace smiled.

'Thanks. It was very good of you. I really appreciate it. Will you stay and have a scone or something?'

Joel glanced at his watch.

'Why not. I'd like that. Home made?'

Grace put a plate of scones in front of him and made another couple of instant coffees.

'My mother made these,' she said over her shoulder. 'She sent me down a batch from the farm to keep in the freezer.'

'You come from a farm? Well, isn't that a coincidence. So do I.'

Grace's astonishment showed in her face as she sat down.

'You're a farmer's boy? I'd never have guessed it.'

Her amazement grew as Joel described his father's sheep farm in the Lake District, how it was now run by his older brother but he enjoyed going back to help in the holidays. A third brother worked in the oil industry and was now in Kuwait. Grace was astounded. She would never have imagined Joel as from a farming background. She would have assumed he came from a line of successful doctors or maybe a wealthy professional family. It just went to show how wrong you could be about someone, but it certainly explained why he was good with his hands.

'I almost went in for veterinary medicine,' he told Grace. 'But in the end I decided it was better if your patients could actually tell you where it hurt.'

'And they're less likely to bite you if you get it wrong,' Grace put in, smiling. 'Although I got a nasty nip from a girl the other day when I was taking out her airway. I moved my hand pretty quick, I can tell you. I never had such a close call when I was helping feed the calves.'

She went on to tell Joel about her parents' farm down in the Cotswolds and the dairy herd that was her father's pride and joy. At last Joel stood up.

'Well, duty calls. Thanks for the coffee and chat, and if you have any more trouble with that lock, let me know, OK?'

He leaned towards her, and before Grace could do anything to prevent it, he kissed her gently on the mouth. Grace's hands flew up, reaching instinctively for him, but he had ended the kiss and was moving away.

'See you later, Grace.'

He walked through the hall and out of the front door, Grace following behind, then with a final wave he went down the path and away. Grace shut the door and leaned against it, waiting for her racing heartbeat to return to normal. And all over a casual little kiss that probably meant nothing to him!

Her lips were still tingling from the touch of his, and when she caught sight of her reflection in the hall mirror she could see that her cheeks were flushed and her eyes abnormally bright. For heaven's sake, she rebuked herself, you're behaving like a silly schoolgirl. Grow up. Grace Bennet!

Over the days that followed, she was conscious that Joel had a discreet but watchful eye on her. It had the effect of making her extra careful with her work, wanting to prove to him that she was getting over the emotional stress of losing Simon.

Joel made no attempt to repeat that kiss, but all the same there was a growing intimacy between them. As far as his work was concerned, his standards were the highest and he had similar expectations of his colleagues, but otherwise Grace found him easy to talk to and, once his reserve was pierced, an entertaining companion. She looked forward to meeting him around the department and he always seemed to have time for a few words. She forgot that other people would notice and were bound to put two and two together and make at least five.

But Ralph brought things to a head. Grace began to notice him watching her with Joel, his gaze worried. One day he came across the two of them in the corridor discussing a patient. Joel's arm was against a doorway, just by Grace's head, and she was smiling up at him. Over his elbow she saw Ralph come into her line of vision and she noticed the concerned way he looked at them. Her heart sank and she excused herself from Joel.

'Sorry, I think Ralph is looking for me.'

Ralph walked down the corridor with her.

'Have you got a minute, Grace? It's my break now, and it's yours, too, am I right?'

'Yes, you are. I was just talking to Joel — to Mr Kirkpatrick — about a patient of his. Have you had a busy morning?'

'Not too bad.'

Ralph told her one or two details of his day, but Grace could tell that he was building up to something, and as they sat down with a couple of coffees she waited to hear it. It was not long in coming.

'Grace, I hope you won't feel I'm interfering,' Ralph said then paused, clearly embarrassed.

'What is it, Ralph?' Grace prompted.

She was pretty sure what she was going to hear, and also that she didn't particularly want to hear it, but it was better to get it out into the open.

'Well, it's you and Joel Kirkpatrick. I can't help noticing that he seems to be taking an interest in you. I mean, nothing too specific, but I'd hate to think of anything getting back to Simon.'

Grace gripped her mug in both hands. She couldn't put it off any longer. She was going to have to tell Ralph about Simon. The news was long overdue.

'Ralph, there's something you need to know.'

Quietly, dispassionately, she told him

the story of her break-up with Simon, and saw his face full of concern.

'I'm very sorry to hear that, Grace, really I am.'

Ralph was silent for a while, frowning down at the table top.

'And does Joel Kirkpatrick know about this?' he asked at last.

'Well, yes, he does. You see, when I heard from Simon I was so upset I nearly walked under Joel's car. Do you remember me telling you about it? And then there was that awful business in Brannigan's. It all came about because I was so shell-shocked. Unfortunately, Joel Kirkpatrick saw me virtually being frog-marched off by the store detective, and, I didn't tell you this at the time, but he was the one who got me off. He went to see the manager, and he explained to her how I'd just had a narrow shave under the wheels of his car. So I had to tell him why I was acting so oddly, otherwise he would have thought I wasn't fit to be let out on my own.'

'I see,' Ralph said. 'So you can't confide in your friends, but you bare your soul to this man.'

'Oh, Ralph, it's not like that. For a start I didn't want to burden you with all this. You've got enough to think about with the baby and everything. And anyway, he knew there was something wrong. I had to tell him, and to be honest he's been very supportive. That's all it is, honestly.'

Ralph was silent for a while, then he turned back to Grace.

'Now that you've told me all this there's something I should say to you. I haven't said anything about it before because I hate spreading tales, but I think in this case I've got to come out with it.'

He put down his coffee cup and turned to face her.

'Grace, I've heard some rather nasty stories about Joel Kirkpatrick. You remember that Maisie used to work at Bart's before we were married?' At Grace's nod he went on, 'Well, she came across him there. She remembered the name when I mentioned it to her. He was only a registrar then, but apparently he was ruthless when it came to using people for his own purposes. He had a long-standing girlfriend then, one of the student nurses. Anyway, to cut a long story short, he eventually decided to move on to better things and ditched her and then started an affair with a married consultant. The poor girl nearly ended up with a nervous breakdown.'

Grace shot him a disbelieving look.

'This sounds like rumour. You know how stories get magnified.'

'Not this one, I'm afraid. That student nurse was Maisie's friend. It finished the girl's career, Grace. She couldn't face nursing after that. I'm afraid there's more to it, as well. The married consultant actually walked out on her husband for our Mr Kirkpatrick, and guess what? He promptly lost interest. The man's a rat, Grace. OK, he's a very good surgeon, don't get me wrong, but if you get involved with him you could be badly hurt. I don't want to see that.'

Grace didn't trust herself to speak. She didn't want to believe Ralph, but she knew him well enough to realise that he wouldn't lie to her. She made one last attempt to justify herself.

'But he's not interested in me, at least, not in that way. He was just concerned, that's all. He wanted to help. He even came and mended my lock for me.'

Ralph shrugged.

'I won't pretend to understand his motives. All I can say is, steer clear of him, especially right now when you're bound to be upset over Simon.'

Grace didn't know what to say. She gave herself a little shake.

'Thanks, Ralph,' she managed at last. 'You've put things into perspective for me. To be honest, I don't want any sort of entanglement with anyone right now. I need time to sort myself out.'

5

It was another busy morning in Recovery, with a lot of pressure on beds. Grace popped into Sister Trainer's office.

'Mrs Wright is ready to go back to the ward, Sister. Shall I phone up for someone?'

She looked up from the paperwork on her desk.

'Fine, it's good to know we have a free bed. There's a road traffic accident coming up that we didn't know about. By the way, how about that chap who had the ear operation? He seemed to have a lot of nausea.'

'Oh, you mean Mr Petersham? He's a dear, trying desperately hard not to be a nuisance, but he was obviously feeling absolutely ghastly when he came round. His sense of balance had completely gone and he said he felt as if he was at sea in a heavy gale, poor man.'

'So what have you done for him?'

'We were advised by Mr Kirkpatrick. The medication he suggested seems to have controlled the nausea, but it's made him a bit dopey. I think we'll have to hang on to him a bit longer.'

'Bother! Oh, well, can't be helped.'

Grace hurried back to the recovery room. She could see Joel Kirkpatrick down at the far end of the room, talking to a newly awakened patient. On impulse Grace made a quick detour into the storeroom. She didn't want to come into contact with Joel more than was strictly necessary.

That talk with Ralph had made a profound effect on her. While she didn't want to believe ill of Joel, she had to admit that it was probably sensible to keep her distance. The split with Simon had left her emotionally vulnerable, even though she was managing to cope with it better than she'd feared at first. But there was no sense in complicating things.

She found what she was looking for and peeped out into the corridor. There was no sign of Joel. His patient was being wheeled back to the ward. Grace took her chance and walked out, only to hear her name called by an all-too-familiar voice.

'Nurse Bennet! Anyone would think you were hiding in there.'

That was uncomfortably near the truth. Grace blushed. She summoned up a suitable noncommittal expression and turned to face Joel who was approaching down the corridor with his usual easy stride.

'Good morning, Mr Kirkpatrick.'

She showed him the packages she was carrying.

'As you can see I was getting some gel for the ward.'

Joel waved a dismissive hand.

'All right, fair enough, but I could be pardoned for thinking you're trying to avoid me, as much as one can in this place. How's things?'

He fell into step with her as they

walked through into the ward. Grace kept up her air of calm politeness even though inwardly she was a quiver of nerves.

'Fine thank you. My front door lock is performing well, and I haven't any other household problems to report.'

'Good, and how about the emotional problems? It seems to be common knowledge now that you and your fiancé have parted for good. No chance of patching things up?'

Grace shot him a sharp glance and warning signals flashed in her mind.

'I don't think this is the time or the place to discuss my personal life, Mr Kirkpatrick,' she stated coolly. 'And now, if you'll excuse me, I have to check on a patient.'

Without waiting to see how he was taking all this she turned away to find Anita watching, wide-eyed.

'I think he fancies you, Grace,' she confided.

'Nonsense!' Grace contradicted sharply. 'He just has a big opinion of himself, that's all.'

'But have you seen the way he watches you? As soon as he comes into Recovery, he looks around for you, and he always comes over for a chat, even if we haven't got one of his patients.'

'Oh, Anita, you're imagining things!'

Grace shook her head in mock despair, but all the same, some of the girl's words struck a chord, reinforcing her own thoughts. She gave herself a little shake.

'Right, Anita, the next patient will be through any minute. Have you checked all the equipment?'

Grace was pleased to have plenty to do, to keep her mind occupied. And she was grateful when, a little later, Bernard Forrester, the young orthopaedic registrar, came through to see how his patient was doing and have a word with her and Anita.

'She's still well under,' Grace said, indicating the sleeping woman. 'I don't expect her to surface for a while yet.'

'OK. Make sure there's plenty of pain

relief available, won't you?' Bernard looked around. 'You're busy this morning.'

'Yes, we are a bit rushed. Mr Kirkpatrick has a whole spate of cases coming in. Young children mostly, for tonsil ops. They're quite hard work because the poor things are often very upset when they come round. I wish I had more time to spend with them.'

Bernard smiled at her.

'I'm sure you're very good with them. If I had to come round from an op I'd love to see you smiling down at me.'

There was a slightly awkward silence, as if he felt he'd said too much. He pushed a few strands of dark hair back under his surgical cap, and cleared his throat as if he were about to make an important announcement. Grace held her breath, trying to keep a straight face.

'How about a coffee in half an hour or so?' he suggested all too casually. 'You're about due a break, aren't you?'

Grace glanced at her watch.

'Well, yes, I am.'

She couldn't help feeling he must have made enquiries about her break time, and the thought amused her.

'All right, I'll see you down there. Reserve me a doughnut, can you, if you get there first?'

'I'll do that.'

Grace expected that Bernard, in his enthusiasm, would be waiting for her in the tea-room complete with doughnut, but in the event she got there first and found the room empty except for one occupant. She paused briefly on the threshold at the sight of Joel Kirkpatrick, leaning back in one of the low chairs. He looked up and their eyes met, holding for a couple of seconds before Grace glanced away. She moved over to the coffee machine and poured herself a cup. A voice came from behind her.

'I've got you that doughnut.'

'What?'

'I heard you ask for a doughnut, so I've got you one.'

'But Bernard was going to get it.'

'So he was,' Joel said smoothly, 'but he was unavoidably delayed. I didn't want you to be disappointed, although I can't approve of your choice. All that saturated fat!'

He shook his head in disapproval. Grace glared at him, annoyed at the cool way he had usurped poor Bernard.

'When I want advice on healthy eating I'll request it,' she retorted. 'Right now I want a doughnut.'

'And here it is.'

Joel indicated the plate in front of him. With an inward sigh of resignation Grace realised she would have to sit with him. Short of ignoring the man or walking out of the room, both of which would be pretty childish, there was nothing else she could do, even though she hated being the victim of such obvious manipulation. So, putting a brave face on it, she walked over and took the seat next to him.

'And now that I have you to myself,' Joel said smoothly, 'there's something I want to ask you. To get straight to the point, I have a couple of tickets for the Easter dance. Would you come with me?'

Grace, her mouth full of doughnut, was unable to reply. Once she'd managed to stop herself choking, she was glad of the chance to think. Overwhelmingly, her first impulse was to accept. Part of her yearned to be swirling round the dance floor in a man's arms, to enjoy herself with him. It had been such a long time since she'd done anything of the kind. But another part, the sensible, sane part, warned her that to accept this invitation would be to embark on a dangerous course that she had no hope of controlling. Ralph's warnings came back to her, recalling the need for caution, and her one thought was to free herself from this disturbing influence.

'Thank you, but — '

'But no? Is this a refusal?' Joel challenged, eyebrows raised. 'Don't tell me you're going with Simon after all?'

Grace began to feel angry. Just who did this man think he was, her personal minder? She put down her coffee cup with a sharp click.

'No, I'm not going with Simon,' she stated flatly. 'It's common knowledge round here that Simon is a thing of the past. Clearly it hasn't occurred to you that someone else might invite me. I wish you'd rid yourself of the idea that you are the only person I know in this hospital.'

Their eyes locked in challenge, but Grace held her ground. She couldn't afford to let him persuade her. Also, she could see that he was mildly taken aback at her refusal, and it annoyed her. Why, he seemed to regard her as his for the taking! Well, she'd soon disabuse him of that! It would do Mr High-And-Mighty Kirkpatrick a bit of good to realise that what he wanted didn't always fall into his lap. But he didn't seem to see it that way.

'Now look here, Grace Bennet,' he

began dangerously but the small insistent sound of his pager suddenly cut through the tense moment.

With a muttered curse Joel stood up. 'We'll continue this conversation later,' he promised. 'Enjoy the doughnut, oh, and by the way, did you know you have jam on the end of your nose?'

In the doorway he nearly collided with Bernard Forrester who was just coming in.

'Oh, Joel, that phone call you told me about wasn't for me after all. It must have been some mistake.'

'Never mind, I've been keeping your seat warm.'

With a wicked wink at Grace, Joel went out, leaving her fuming. Bernard came over, full of apologies for keeping her waiting. She hardly heard him, her thoughts were in such turmoil. In a moment of madness she'd practically told Joel that she was going to the dance with someone else, and sooner or later he was bound to discover that she wasn't.

'So what do you think, Grace?' Bernard was saying.

'I'm sorry? What was that?'

'The dance. I just asked if you'd like to come to the dance with me.'

Grace stared at him. Suddenly, in the unprepossessing form of the cheery Bernard Forrester she saw a knight in shining armour coming to rescue her.

'Why, Bernard, thank you. I'd love to go with you.'

* * *

St Margaret's Hospital Easter Dance was one of the high spots of the social calendar in the town. Well-organised by a social committee, it invariably raised a lot of money for hospital funds, besides providing an evening's entertainment for the hard-working staff. But it was not quite as entertaining as Grace had hoped, because, unfortunately, Bernard was proving something of a disaster as a partner.

He had firmly ensconced himself and

Grace at a table of middle-aged doctors and their wives and seemed determined to talk shop all evening. In fact, Grace thought to herself, I don't know why he bothered to invite me at all. He could just as well have come by himself.

Sister Trainer swept past on the dance floor with her husband. Grace surveyed all the dresses that swirled past her. She felt more and more confident of her own choice of dress. The Brannigan's blue silk gown was exactly right, just dressy enough without being ostentatious. It was a small comfort for her to know she'd got that right, even if the rest of the evening wasn't a success.

As she thought this over, Grace caught sight of a couple just entering the room. She couldn't see them too clearly because of the pass of people in the way, but there was enough of a buzz at their entrance to make her aware that this was someone special. She saw the woman first, a striking-looking redhead, tall and slim, wearing a vivid green dress, cut extremely low, with an extravagantly flared skirt that swirled about her as she walked. No wonder she was attracting more than her fair share of attention.

Grace wondered who her partner could be. She shifted her gaze to the man behind the auburn-haired girl, and drew in her breath sharply. Well, she might have guessed it. It was Joel Kirkpatrick! The shock of seeing him hit her like a physical blow, even though she'd known he would be there and had prepared herself for seeing him with someone else. She gripped the edge of the table in front of her, willing herself to stay calm, show no emotion, take no notice. After all, what Joel Kirkpatrick chose to do was no concern of hers.

'Drink up, there. You're lagging behind!'

Grace snapped back to reality as a glass was put down in front of her to join the untouched drink that was already there. One of the other doctors had just stood another round and had brought her a second glass of punch to follow her first one. Obediently Grace picked up the nearest glass and took a long drink. The punch was pleasantly flavoured with just a tang of alcohol in the background. Not usually a drinker, she was pleased to find something relatively innocuous. Ice cubes and chopped fruit floated in it. Yes, it was very palatable, and most refreshing in the hot, crowded room.

'I notice Joel Kirkpatrick has arrived.'

Bernard turned to her during a lull in the medical conversation.

'Oh, yes?'

Grace tried not to sound too concerned.

'Did you see his partner?' one of the wives enthused. 'What a stunner! Don't they make a wonderful couple. That man is so good-looking!'

Right on cue, Joel and his partner waltzed past. Grace noted without surprise that they both were skilful dancers and they were talking animatedly. As Grace saw the way the girl looked up into Joel's eyes, the breath caught in her throat. That could have been me, she found herself thinking. She wondered if Joel had seen her here sitting with this sober group, and if so, what he thought. Probably he'd find it very amusing, that she'd turned down the chance of being his partner in order to sit and discuss medical ethics all evening.

But at least this is safe, she told herself. And if I'm not having quite the most fascinating evening of my life, well that's the price you pay for security.

The evening dragged on. Grace finished her second glass of punch and was duly presented with a third. There was half an hour to go to the buffet supper. Then there was a stir at the table. Someone was coming to join them. With a sick feeling of inevitability Grace looked up and saw Joel and his partner coming over. People were moving round to make space, and the girl was actually going to sit next to her. She summoned up a smile, but before she could say anything one of the more vocal wives took charge.

'I'll introduce everybody.'

She went round the group, naming names, and then asked Joel's partner her name.

'I'm Honor Delaney. I'm afraid I'm nothing to do with the world of medicine. I'm a freelance artist.'

'Oh, how fascinating! Tell us about it!'

So Honor described her work to her interested audience, while at the other end of the table, Joel was drawn into the men's conversation. Apart from a brief greeting to the assembled company, he did not acknowledge Grace, but she hadn't expected anything else. To her surprise, she found herself liking Honor. Although most of the women were prepared to be impressed by her, she seemed genuinely self-deprecating and inclined to play down her artistic career.

'It's not that glamorous, really,' she told them. 'I do portraits, and pets are very popular. I've just had a commission to work on a children's book, too, but it's just a job, just like anything else and at times it can be just as routine. Whereas I've often thought it must be fascinating to work in a hospital with all that life and death drama, and those handsome doctors!'

There was a murmur of amused dissent from the women in the group, most of whom were married to doctors, now middle-aged and balding!

'But you should know about handsome doctors!' someone said. 'You've certainly done well for yourself tonight!'

'Oh, Joel?' Honor smiled. 'Yes, he is a dear, isn't he? We go back a long way.'

Grace had heard enough. All the time Joel had been casting lures in her direction, he actually had an on-going relationship with Honor! It looked like he hadn't changed much since those days that Ralph had told her about.

'Shall we go for something to eat?' Bernard suggested suddenly.

Grace winced. The thought of food

made her feel queasy.

'No, you go on and save me a place,' she suggested. 'I'd like to sit for a bit. I'm quite hot.'

'All right then. I'll go and join the Mortimers. You come along when you're ready.'

The window was open and a cooling breeze played on Grace's heated skin. She was grateful for it, and for a few moment's peace to herself. Hopefully she'd soon feel better and be able to join the others for supper, though to be honest she doubted whether she could manage more than a few mouthfuls of food. Why was she feeling so awful? Was it just the sight of Joel and Honor enjoying each other's company, or was there more to it than that?

A shadow fell across her and she glanced up with a sinking feeling, expecting Bernard to be exhorting her to hurry up, but the dark face looking down at her in concern belonged to Joel Kirkpatrick.

'You don't look too good, Grace.

How are you feeling?'

Grace raised her chin to meet his assessing gaze.

'I'm quite hot. It's so crowded in here, it makes me thirsty.'

She picked up the glass, meaning to finish off the fruit punch, but Joel reached forward and took the glass away, preventing her from drinking.

'Then that's the last thing you want. That stuff's lethal.'

'What? But it's only fruit juice, and a bit of wine or something.'

'You must be joking! The medical students cooked this up. There's a hefty dose of vodka in there.' His expression darkened. 'You don't mean to tell me Bernard Forrester has been letting you knock back that stuff all evening? How many have you had?'

Grace tried to think back.

'Three or four,' she hazarded.

'Good heavens! I'm surprised you're still upright. The thing is, what to do now?'

He gestured to a passing waiter who

instantly came over.

'Get this lady a drink of cold water, can you? Right now, please. Now, Grace, we're going to get you home.'

Grace was beginning to feel really annoyed. Once again Joel was calmly assuming he could take charge of her life. She was trying to summon up a suitably cutting remark, when a familiar voice intruded.

'Grace! Where have you been hiding all evening? I'd ask you for a dance, but we're just going. Maisie's already out in the car. You know how it is with these pregnant women, can't stand the pace!'

'Ralph, you look very smart.'

Grace summoned up her reserves of control to return his cheerful smile even though she was beginning to feel ghastly. Fortunately she was saved from having to say much by Joel who cut across Ralph's reply.

'You say you're going? Right now, before supper?'

'Yes, Maisie needs her beauty sleep.'

'Well, that solves our little problem.

Grace isn't feeling too great and she would like to go home. Perhaps you could give her a lift if it's not too far out of your way.'

'Of course, we'd be glad to, but what about Bernard?'

'I'll take care of that. How about it, Grace?'

Grace started to protest. Really it was too much the way this man calmly assumed he could order her about! But then the room swayed and lurched in the most alarming fashion and she reluctantly had to concede that Joel was quite right. The only sensible thing to do was to go home.

With a stilted, 'Thank you,' she got to her feet and accepted the support of Ralph's arm out of the hall to the car, where Maisie was waiting. Once again it seemed that she was beholden to Joel Kirkpatrick and it was definitely not a feeling she enjoyed.

6

Fortunately Grace was on a later shift the following day. Even so she definitely didn't feel too well when she arrived at work, and it looked like being a busy day, too. Her first job was to attend to a burns patient newly back from theatre. The consultant, David Griffith, who had carried out the skin grafts, came to have a look at his patient.

'Be sure to keep a close watch on his fluid output and feel free to offer him plenty to drink. He should do all right, he's a big strong lad, but he's been quite badly burned,' he said to Grace.

He put down the fluid chart and turned back to Grace.

'You can't be feeling too good yourself today,' he commented with a smile. 'Joel did you a good turn last night, I hear. It says something for his presence of mind that he was able to

106

tear his attention away from that Honor. What a girl! He tried to tell me some story that she was his brother's girlfriend, would you believe. The brother's in Kuwait, has been for over a year, I believe. Don't think he'll stand much of a chance with Honor when he gets back.'

Grace pursed her lips, remembering the way Honor had smiled up into Joel's face as they danced. This revelation from David fitted in all too well with what she'd seen, and with the character of Joel Kirkpatrick as revealed by Ralph. It seemed that he was entirely without scruples. Behind her she heard the consultant move away, and breathed a sigh of relief.

Grace was on duty checking patients in for the rest of the day. Mostly it was routine work, asking their names, did they know what their operation involved, and filling in as much detail about it for them as she judged advisable. Several of them were Joel's patients, for small operations, so it looked like his afternoon was just as routine as hers.

Grace had decided she had to speak to him, to let him know that she wanted no further interference from him in her life, especially now that he was involved with Honor. Her chance arrived when he came to have a few words with a newly-admitted patient. As soon as he had finished chatting and reassuring the small boy, Grace attracted his attention.

'Mr Kirkpatrick, have you a spare moment?'

Her tone was cool and reserved, but inwardly she was very tense, her pulses thudding in her ears. She was about to do something which couldn't happen to Joel very often — she was going to tell him to go away and mind his own business. She hoped she could do it with sufficient conviction.

Joel glanced up at the clock at the end of the room.

'Yes, you're in luck as it happens. I'm running well ahead of time. How about a nice civilised cup of tea?'

'What I have to say won't take that long, Mr Kirkpatrick, and I'd rather say it in private. Perhaps we could use Sister's office. It's empty just now.'

Joel raised his eyebrows in mild surprise but he followed her into the small office. Once there he sat irreverently on Sister Trainer's desk, one long leg swinging, and waited for her to begin. Grace took a deep breath and plunged straight in.

'About last night.'

'Don't mention it.' Joel waved a dismissive hand. 'I was glad to be able to help. How are you feeling, by the way? I bet you had a sore head this morning.'

Grace mentally counted to ten. This conversation was not going the way she intended it to. She made an effort to regain the initiative.

'Sorry, but I do intend to mention it. You had no right to do what you did.'

Joel's dark eyebrows met in a frown.

'I don't quite read you, Grace. You're saying you resent the fact that I got you

109

safe home when you were practically legless.'

'That's not true! Yes, I'd overdone it on the punch, but that wasn't my fault.'

'Fair enough. But, Grace — '

'Yes?'

'Stop waving your arms about like that. People are staring.'

Grace glanced out through the glass panes into the recovery room. True enough, several interested faces were looking in their direction. She'd forgotten just how public Sister Trainer's office was. She swallowed hard, and tried to look as though this were merely a routine discussion of medical matters.

'Look, I'm not objecting to the way you got Ralph to run me home. OK, I'm grateful for that, thank you, but what I really do object to is the way you seem to want to run my life for me. I don't need you hovering in the background like some sort of guardian angel.'

Despite herself she couldn't help collapsing in sudden laughter at the very idea of Joel dangling in mid-air wearing a white smock and a halo. He seemed to share her amusement and his serious expression vanished, to be replaced by a broad grin.

'You really have a gift for words, don't you, Grace? But I take your point. All the same, now that you have so lyrically expressed your opinion, how about you listen to mine? There are one or two things I want to get straight between us. I'm not trying to be a guardian angel, or some sort of big brother to you, Grace.'

'Then what are you trying to be?'

His voice darkened. It sent a shiver of awareness running through her.

'Can't you guess? I know it started with me simply wanting to help you out of a jam, just as a concerned colleague, but there's more to it than that now. Grace, I want to be someone special in your life. Believe me, you are in mine already.'

Grace felt as though all the breath had been knocked out of her. Only by an almost superhuman effort could she prevent her face contorting into a spasm of disbelief. He couldn't be saying this! He couldn't mean it! Seconds passed before she could say anything, and even then her voice sounded in her ears as a hoarse croak. She cleared her throat and tried again.

'But what about Honor, the girl you took to the dance?'

'Honor?' Joel's tone was dismissive. 'What about her? You don't think there's anything between us, do you? There isn't. In Ben's absence I took her to the dance, that's all. I could just as well ask you about Bernard Forrester.'

Grace steeled herself to stay calm even though her mind was a chaos of conflicting emotions. She was very much aware that her every action was visible through the glass to anyone who cared to look. Thank heaven they couldn't be overheard.

'Grace,' Joel was insistent now, 'we must talk. I'd like to come round sometime.'

Before he could say anything more, there was a sharp rap on the glass window, and one of the other staff nurses was seen gesticulating worriedly. Grace's hand flew to her mouth.

'Oh, I must fly! It's an emergency. Sorry, this will have to wait.'

She was already halfway through the door as she spoke, not waiting to judge Joel's reaction. As soon as she was back in the recovery room she realised what was happening. One of the post-operative patients was haemorrhaging badly. Sister Trainer immediately issued Grace with orders and immediately she was automatically carrying out her important duties.

The surgeon arrived together with the anaesthetist and had a hurried consultation before agreeing the patient had better go back to theatre for the problem to be sorted out. As soon as Grace had got the patient set up, a porter came to wheel the man back through to theatre. Everyone could sit back and take a breather.

Grace looked up and down the room. There was no sign of Joel. It looked as though he'd decided to make himself scarce while the emergency was being dealt with or maybe he'd been called back into theatre. Either way there was no chance of continuing their conversation, and she had no way of knowing exactly what he'd been going to say to her. But one thing was clear — she hadn't heard the end of it.

He had something important to say to her. Perhaps after all he and Honor had decided to go their separate ways. Perhaps the way was clear for a new relationship. A quicksilver dart of excitement shot through her before she could prevent it, but there was no point in speculating. She would have to hear him out and then make up her mind.

She didn't see Joel again all that shift. After the excitement of the emergency the rest of the day passed without incident, but after her late night at the dance she felt quite tired. The night staff came on at half past eight and it was a relief when she eventually arrived home and could shut the door behind her.

She had sat for a while, eating a pizza and trying to be interested in the chat show that was on TV, when there was a brisk knock at the front door. Her heart did a crazy somersault. Joel? She'd had no time to think straight. Nerves on edge, she went to the door, and opened it.

Grace closed her eyes, hardly believing what she saw, and then opened them again. She wasn't imagining it. It was Simon who stood there! She tried to pull her scattered thoughts together. It was the unexpectedness of it that hit her so forcefully. Somehow she'd never expected to see him again, and now here he was on her doorstep, just as if he'd never been away.

'Hello, Grace.' His voice was quiet, apologetic even. 'May I come in?'

She could hardly refuse.

'Sure — er, yes, do.'

She pulled the door wide and stood

to one side to let Simon go past her. He paused for a moment, and she wondered if he was going to kiss her. She knew she didn't want him to. Something in her manner must have communicated itself to him because after a second's hesitation, he smiled ruefully and walked on past into the sitting-room. Grace followed.

'Do sit down,' she invited after a brief hesitation. 'Can I get you a coffee or something?'

'No thanks.'

Grace took a seat opposite and for a few moments there was a yawning silence. She didn't know what to say and it looked as though Simon was having a similar problem. At last he broke the silence.

'I'm sorry to burst in on you like this, but I had to come while I was over in England. It hasn't worked out, Grace, Dagmar and I, I mean. It just wasn't right, I can see that now. I want you back.'

Grace stared. She could hardly

believe what she was hearing. After all the pain, all the heartache, he had the gall to come and sit there and say calmly that he wanted her back, and expect her to come running into his arms. What did he take her for? Something of her feelings must have shown in her face for Simon swallowed hard and put up a hand defensively.

'I can understand if you feel angry with me,' he said. 'I've been a fool, and I deserve anything you care to call me.'

He sounded, Grace thought, for all the world like a child who had thrown away its favourite toy in a fit of pique and now wanted it back. But all the same she couldn't help feeling very sorry for him. The regret and self-reproach in his tone was authentic. She felt herself weakening. A two-year relationship couldn't be cast aside just like that.

'Oh, Simon, do you realise what you're asking? To rebuild our relationship from nothing?'

'We had a good relationship. Everybody thought so.'

'I suppose they did,' Grace said slowly. 'From the outside we were the perfect couple. Only there was something missing. We lacked — oh, I don't know — fire, passion, excitement. We had got too predictable. We took each other for granted.'

Simon's eyes widened.

'Do you really think so? I hadn't realised, but how come you think like this, Grace? Don't say you've met someone else.'

Grace hesitated only fractionally.

'I've met lots of people,' she said lightly, 'but who's to say if any one of them is Mr Right? No, I'm still footloose and fancy free.'

She hoped she sounded more convincing than she felt. She watched Simon guardedly to see how he was taking this. He appeared to be relieved.

'I'm glad,' he said. 'And now I want to know if there's still room in your life for me. Will you forgive me, Grace? I'm truly sorry. Can we start again where we left off? I need you so much.'

An imperious knocking interrupted him. Grace jumped, her first impression one of profound relief, replaced almost immediately by a sudden sick dread in the pit of her stomach. There was only one person this could be. Her mouth was dry. For a couple of mad seconds she thought of ignoring the knock, but no, that was silly. The light was on for a start, and Simon would think it very odd if she didn't answer the door. And anyway, it might not be him, she thought to herself. They hadn't fixed anything definite, after all. It might be a neighbour, or someone from work.

'Excuse me a minute,' she said as casually as she could, getting up and going out of the room.

In the few seconds it took her to cross the hall to the front door she went through feverish mental preparation, but all the same when she opened the door and saw Joel standing there, the blood drained from her face. Her knees felt weak. She leaned against the doorpost for support.

'Hello, Grace. Not surprised to see me, I hope. We have unfinished business, I seem to remember.'

'Joel, I — '

Grace cast a frantic look behind her. If only Simon weren't there. Everything was about as wrong as it could be. She couldn't cope with all this. She wanted space.

'I don't know that it's all that convenient just now,' she began, stalling for time, but Joel interrupted.

'I happen to know you're on late shift again tomorrow, and I also know that you ate practically nothing all day. So I thought this might be a good occasion to take you out for that meal I promised. We can talk over dinner and a glass of wine. There's a good new restaurant opened in the old market place. How about it?'

'Er, well — '

Grace was completely at a loss. Then she cringed inwardly, for behind her a voice rang out and her hopes crumbled into dust.

'Who is it, Grace? Not some doorstep salesman, I hope.'

Simon appeared through from the sitting-room and stood behind her, peering out at the visitor. She saw Joel's eyes widen for an instant, then his gaze dropped to her arm, where Simon was holding her in the protective gesture she remembered of old. She pulled away but it was too late. Joel had seen the movement. She felt him tense. His assessing gaze went from Grace to Simon and back again. His stare was flint-hard.

'No, not a doorstep salesman,' he said smoothly, 'but an equally unwelcome guest, it seems. You are the long-lost Simon, I presume, returned like the prodigal son. I wish you joy in your reunion. I can see why you were so reluctant to let me in, Grace. Don't let me interrupt you.'

And with that he turned on his heel and walked down the garden path without a backwards glance. Grace closed the door and rested her head on it for an instant. She felt completely numb. Well, it's for the best, a little voice said. Remember what Ralph had to say — you're better off out of it. But there was absolutely no comfort in the cold logic. Grace couldn't remember ever feeling quite so bereft.

'Grace, Grace!' Simon pressed her but it was an effort to focus on what he was saying. 'Who was that?'

'Oh, no-one in particular. Just a colleague from work. He probably wanted to discuss something.'

Simon frowned.

'I don't think I know him.'

Grace led the way back into the sitting-room, moving automatically.

'That's because he's new. He's an ENT surgeon.'

'A consultant?'

Simon watched through the window as Joel's sleek black car accelerated away down the road.

'Yes.'

Grace sat down, staring ahead of her. What might have happened if Simon hadn't been there? Where would she be right now? In Joel's arms? She shuddered, trying to put the vision out of her mind.

'He seemed rather annoyed to find me here,' Simon went on. 'If I didn't know you better I'd say you were being rather economical with the truth, as they say. He is someone special, isn't he?'

Grace made a hopeless gesture.

'Well, OK. He was sort of interested in me, yes, but it wouldn't have worked. His reputation isn't exactly the best.'

Simon came back over to the sofa where Grace sat, fighting back the tears. He put an arm round her, and she didn't resist, knowing that his sympathy and concern for her were genuine.

'Look, Grace, if I've just screwed things up for you, tell me. You know I want you back. My feelings for you haven't changed, but if yours for me have, well, just say the word.'

Grace shook her head.

'I just don't know, Simon. Don't rush me. Maybe in time, oh, I just don't know.'

After Simon left, she didn't feel sleepy, so she picked up a copy of the Nursing Times and leafed through the pages. The articles failed to engross her, but an advert did, for a job at an infirmary in the North of England, a small town, Penrigg, on the edge of the Lake District, where a new recovery unit was just being set up in the expanded local hospital. The job was for a staff nurse in Recovery, very similar to what she was doing, except that it would mean a complete change of scene. She could sell up, start afresh, leave the old memories behind, get well away from one particular ENT surgeon.

Before she could change her mind, Grace wrote off an answer to the ad, then went out and dropped it in the post box on the corner.

7

Over the days that followed, Grace saw hardly anything of Joel. Of course at certain times she came across him in Recovery, but he was meticulously polite to her, nothing more. He gave Grace no opportunity for any private conversation whatsoever. He was his old remote self.

Grace was also aware of Joel's growing involvement with Honor. One day as she was walking in through the hospital gates she had to jump sharply to one side to avoid being mowed down by Joel Kirkpatrick's car as it swept into the carpark. The car stopped a little farther along and Honor leaned out through the driver's window to apologise.

'It's Grace, isn't it? I really am sorry. I took the corner too wide. I'm borrowing the car for the day but I had to run Joel into work first.'

At that point Grace had noticed Joel sitting in the passenger seat looking suitably tight-lipped. Grace had wondered how he felt about entrusting his valuable car to such an erratic driver, but she was more impressed by the insight into Joel's and Honor's relationship. Still, it was no concern of hers, although she felt a pang of sympathy for his absent brother, Honor's supposed boyfriend. She wondered how much he knew about the situation out in Kuwait.

Anita, the young student nurse, had moved on to a spell in theatre so Grace saw something of her from time to time as theatre and recovery room staff shared a dining-room, and Anita, when she wasn't chatting with other student nurses, often came to sit with Grace when their meal breaks coincided. Distressingly for Grace she liked to talk about Joel. She had evidently got a crush on him.

'You should see him operating!' she enthused. 'These ear operations are so fiddly some of them, but he just chats away as if it was nothing! But if there's anything not quite right he makes you feel terrible. I got in a muddle over counting the swabs and he was so cutting! But he's really gorgeous. The way he looks at you over the top of his mask just sends a shiver down my spine!'

Grace smiled, tight-lipped. Anita's prattle, though harmless enough, was an unwelcome reminder of Joel's magnetism. Yes, she could imagine his dark eyes smiling down at her, his long-fingered hands moving with skilled certainty at his work. She could hear his voice, reflecting his mood, whether playful or critical. Oh, dear, how long would it take for this vision to fade from her mind?

She made an excuse and got up, but, oh, horror, in the doorway she almost collided with Joel himself coming in. She made a frantic leap to one side, anything to avoid physical contact. Oh, no, she thought wretchedly, I can't go on like this! I feel so awkward, yet he obviously doesn't want to talk to me. What can I do to clear the air? I don't want it to be like this. We should at least be at ease with each other.

There was something else to be thought about, too, something she didn't want to reveal to anyone just yet. The hospital in Penrigg had written inviting her for an interview, in fact they sounded very impressed by her qualifications and experience. That would be the best solution, if she could only get that job and move right away, away from Joel Kirkpatrick and his disturbing influence.

The following day, Grace arrived late for her shift. There was just time to get into her surgical greens and get out on to the ward without even time for a word with Sister Trainer. All the same, there seemed to be an atmosphere in Recovery. There was a definite buzz about the place, and Grace wasn't sure what it could be. She made a mental note to find out as she greeted her first patient. The lady was middle-aged, and was having nodules removed from her vocal chords. As a keen amateur singer, she was naturally very anxious about the outcome and Grace had sent a student nurse to ask if Mr Kirkpatrick would come and speak to the patient if he had a moment.

She prepared herself mentally for their meeting, but all the same her heart thudded when she saw his tall figure, shrouded in his theatre grown, appear in the doorway. She managed to keep all emotion out of her voice.

'Here's Mr Kirkpatrick now, Mrs Thoresby, he'll tell you all you need to know,' she said.

She stood back while Joel had a few reassuring words with the woman. She admired the way he calmly explained the procedure that was to be carried out. He made no attempt to skate over the discomfort she would probably experience when she awoke but emphasised his optimism as to the outcome. He really had a gift for putting people at their ease, Grace noted. She couldn't help comparing it with the turmoil he aroused in her own emotions.

'And when you come round, you'll find Grace here at your bedside,' he finished, motioning Grace to come forward. 'She's one of our most efficient Recovery nurses. You'll be in very capable hands. Make sure you're there,' he whispered to Grace as he left the patient's side to return to theatre. 'I hope I haven't messed up Sister Trainer's staff schedule.'

'I'm sure it will be all right.' Then, seeing him start to walk away, she raised her voice slightly. 'Mr Kirkpatrick, can I have a minute or two of your time, if it's convenient?'

He turned and looked at her, his gaze assessing. For a bleak moment she thought he was going to refuse, but then he appeared to relent.

'All right, will now do? I haven't long, mind.'

'OK. But please could we go somewhere just a little more private?'

Joel inclined his head briefly.

'Let's try the tea-room. It should be empty right now.'

He turned and led the way down the corridor, Grace following and trying to collect her thoughts. She'd have to be quick and to the point and she desperately hoped she'd say the right things. She couldn't help feeling it wasn't the best of moments to choose, in fact for whatever reason, Joel very definitely looked under considerable strain. But she would have to make the best of it. Once inside the dining-room, which fortunately was deserted, she faced up to him.

'Joel, these last few days have been awful, ever since you came round and found Simon at my house.'

'Are you surprised?' Joel's tone was bitter. 'How do you expect me to react when I find I've stumbled on to a cosy little reconciliation scene? After all the pronouncements about Simon being a thing of the past, did you expect me to stop and drink your joint health?'

Grace flushed.

'Of course not! But I don't see why you have to treat me like a social leper. Why can't we just be friends?'

Joel stood glaring down at her, just inches away. She could easily have reached out and touched him, but she kept her hands firmly by her sides. Outside in the corridor a trolley clattered past.

'Oh, all right.' Joel flung his arms wide in a despairing gesture. 'Yes, you're right, I've been behaving like an idiot. Truth is, as you probably know, I've got something else on my mind right now. I guess I'm not in the best frame of mind to be Mr Nice Guy, but I'll try. What do you want from me, just say and I'll try to deliver.'

His words were wounding, deeply wounding. Tears pricked at Grace's eyelids, but she blinked them back.

'I just want us to be friends, Joel,' she said. 'It means a lot to me.'

Joel stared down at her for several heart-stopping seconds. Finally he said quietly, 'And it means a great deal to me, Grace. Over the last few days I've begun to realise just how much.'

He turned and looked out of the window, shoulders hunched. Grace could hardly believe what she was hearing. The great Joel Kirkpatrick, renowned for his self-assurance, was actually confessing to being vulnerable. She was consumed by a feeling of great compassion and tenderness as she went forward and gently touched his arm.

'I'm sorry, Joel,' she whispered, her voice a mere thread. 'Believe me, I didn't want to hurt you.'

Then, wordlessly, Joel turned and reached out for her and gathered her into his arms. Grace sank helplessly against him.

'All right, if that's what you want,' he said, and then, as she'd known he would, he kissed her, his mouth coming down on hers in a gentle but highly sensual motion that left her weak and wanting more.

But then, abruptly, reality dawned on

Grace, and with it the realisation of how passionately she had responded to that kiss. Shame flooded through her. That reaction seemed to belie everything she'd just said. She moved away, her cheeks flaming.

'I'm sorry. That shouldn't have happened.'

'Shouldn't it? Why not, Grace? I think it should. You're deceiving yourself if you think there's nothing between us. You've just shown me that there is.'

He stepped forward and perhaps would have taken her in his arms again, but Grace moved round to the other side of a table. She took a deep, calming breath, gripping the edge of the table for support.

'That's not fair, Joel. You did that on purpose. You wanted me to respond like that, but it doesn't change anything. And let me ask you a straight question. Where do you stand with Honor? What does she think about all this?'

Joel started to say something, then stopped suddenly, running a hand through his hair, pushing it back from his brow. He seemed at a loss.

'Honor! I suppose you've heard about the mess she's in?' Then, seeing Grace's blank expression, he went on, 'You know what our relationship is, even though everyone else seems to choose not to believe it.'

Seeing her confused expression, he stepped forward and took both her hands in his, kneading the palms with his long fingers. His eyes met hers, steady and serious.

'I want you to understand this, Grace, though you could be forgiven if you don't. God knows, everyone else seems to have the wrong idea. You see — ' but before he could go any further, his name echoed through the tea-room.

Sister Trainer had appeared round the door, her face anxious. On seeing Joel and Grace, who had immediately sprung apart, her expression changed. But not, as Grace would have expected, to surprised interest at seeing the two of them together in a pretty compromising situation, or gleeful anticipation at the thought of a good story with which to regale her colleagues. No, Joyce Trainer was looking at them with horror, and as her gaze swept over Joel, Grace was amazed to recognise something like contempt. When she spoke again, Sister's voice was like ice.

'Mr Kirkpatrick, there's an emergency. Can you come, please? Grace, I think we'll need you, too.'

She stood aside to let Joel pass, then fell into step beside Grace, panting slightly as they hurried through the corridor back to Recovery. Grace was at a loss. Why had Joyce looked at Joel like that? It was as if he was something that had just crawled out from under a stone. She didn't have the chance to question Sister Trainer immediately for they were kept busy with the emergency patient.

It was only later when the patient was in theatre and things had calmed down that Grace was able to snatch a quick

136

word with Sister Trainer. Even then she could tell that the older woman was evasive and upset.

'Joyce, what is it? There's something the matter, something about Joel. Can you tell me?'

Sister Trainer's glance was full of compassion.

'Grace, oh, Grace, get out of it while you still can. You want nothing to do with that man.'

'But what is it?'

Sister Trainer shook her head.

'Grace have you seen the list of patients for theatre this afternoon?'

'No, not yet. Why?'

'Well, I suggest you go and look. Then you'll know what I'm talking about.'

With that, she hurried off, leaving Grace mystified, staring after her. Eventually she gave herself a little shake. Better go and check that list and then perhaps all would be revealed. When she got hold of the list, she realised immediately. This must be what

Joel had wanted to say to her. Her mind struggled to assimilate what had happened, but she had the odd feeling of being a spectator, standing outside herself, watching a woman in surgical greens staring at a list of patients.

The floor swayed under her feet, then ever so slowly righted itself. She didn't want to believe what she saw there, but there was no denying the words in red added between the neatly typed letters. Miss Honor Delaney had been an emergency admission, with an ectopic pregnancy. She was probably in theatre now, and later Grace would see her, if not care for her, in Recovery. That must have been what was on Joel's mind. That was what he'd meant when he'd said Honor needed her help.

Slowly the full horror of the situation dawned on her. It was obvious, wasn't it? Honor had been carrying Joel's baby! And yet, such a short time ago, Joel had told Grace there was nothing serious between himself and Honor! Ralph's warnings were brought back forcibly to Grace's unwilling brain. As she walked back to Recovery, scarcely seeing where she was going, she tried to make some sense of the ghastly situation. On the face of it, Joel Kirkpatrick was beneath contempt.

Honor was brought through to Recovery half an hour later. Grace volunteered to nurse her.

'She knows me, Sister. It might comfort her a bit to see a familiar face.'

Sister Trainer had looked strangely at her, no doubt wondering why she was making a martyr of herself, but Grace had felt better for it. She was trying to prove to herself that she could cope with this situation, even though she was slowly dying inside. Honor looked pale, her face pinched. She was breathing without oxygen when she was brought through and the anaesthetist who accompanied her, knowing nothing of the situation, was cheerful.

'Everything went smoothly. She shouldn't be long in coming round. Might be a bit tearful though.'

Mechanically, Grace set about the usual procedure, going through the list of checks with the anaesthetist. She tried to convince herself that Honor was just an ordinary patient. It should make no difference, only it did.

At last, Honor opened her eyes and tried to focus. She moved her head restlessly, and pulled at the sheets.

'What's happening? Where am I?'

Grace took hold of her hand, automatically checking the pulse.

'Everything's all right, Honor. It's me, Grace, remember me?'

'Grace. Yes, I remember, and, oh, no, now I remember. The baby, I've lost the baby!'

Tears formed slowly and started to trickle down her cheeks. Grace felt an answering prickle behind her own eyelids, but she blinked the tears away.

'I'm sorry, Honor,' she said quietly.

No sense in coming out with the usual platitudes about there would be other babies. She knew from experience that this sort of approach was never a comfort. Grace sat quietly holding Honor's hand while Honor lay with eyes closed. At last Honor stirred.

'Please, could I see him? Joel, I mean.'

Grace hesitated. 'I don't know. He'll be operating.'

'Oh, of course.'

Honor closed her eyes again, and Grace did the same, trying unsuccessfully to shut out the pain that tore at her heart. Of all the cruel situations ever devised this must be the worst. And then she was conscious of a movement at her side, and she knew who it would be even before she opened her eyes. It was Joel.

'Honor, I'm here.'

His voice sounded choked as he took Honor's frail hand in his. Grace quietly got up and left them alone. How she managed to last out until the end of her shift she couldn't afterwards say. But when she got home the first thing she did was write a letter agreeing to go north for the interview. She was going to do her damnedest to get that job and as soon as she could she would be away. Away from St Margaret's, from Honor, and most of all, away from Joel Kirkpatrick.

8

Grace got the job in Penrigg. She was told immediately following her interview, and the sense of relief was overwhelming. She had a month's notice to work at St Margaret's, but she had three weeks' leave due to her so in effect she only had one week to complete.

There were so many things to do — put her little house on the market, arrange for a place in the nurses' hostel up north while she looked for somewhere more permanent, sort out somewhere for her furniture. It was difficult breaking the news, so many people were sorry to see her go. So it was at the end of an emotionally fraught day that she settled down to some of the nitty-gritty of the move, going out into the garden to do a general tidy.

She didn't normally have much time for anything beyond keeping the grass cut and the shrub borders weeded, but some of the bushes needed a drastic cut-back if the plot was to look tidy. She borrowed a pair of clippers from a neighbour and set to work. She was so engrossed in her task that she didn't hear the car stop outside her gate, or the footsteps that came up the path, so the sound of her name called out made her jump. A large piece of forsythia descended on her head in a confused tangle.

'Oh, see what you've made me do! Oh, Joel.'

He stood quite still, one hand propped against the porch, the other shoved in his trouser pocket. His wide mouth was quirked in a half smile, his head slightly tilted to one side as he watched her disengage herself from the forsythia. Grace couldn't utter another word. She felt distinctly ridiculous.

'Let me do that.'

Strong hands relieved her of the

cutters, and for a few moments Joel worked away reaching up to the topmost branches of the shrub. When he had finished, Grace had to admit that he'd made a good job of it. The damage done by her ill-advised chop had been repaired and the bush, though smaller than she'd intended, was a neat, regular shape. Joel stood back and examined it with a critical eye.

'I think that will have to do. Any more for the knife?'

'No, that's about all here at the front, thank you.'

Silence descended. Grace couldn't think what to say. She wasn't going to be talked out of leaving if that's what his purpose was in coming. She didn't want to ask after Honor, it would be too painful. She didn't want to invite him in, but that was plainly what he had in mind.

'I came to wish you all the best, Grace. I heard you were leaving and I hoped we might part on a friendly note,' he said.

No attempt at complicated explanations or excuses followed. It looked like it would just be a calm, dignified farewell, the sort of thing she'd wanted all along. She could just about cope with that.

'Come on in, then, I'll put the kettle on.'

She walked ahead of him into the house, determined to keep her distance. The old feelings of attraction were still there, just as strong, but she couldn't let him see it. Once in the kitchen, she busied herself with preparing coffee and brought out a packet of chocolate biscuits.

'I hope you appreciate the honour,' she said jokingly as she tipped a few on to a plate. 'It's not often these things appear in my kitchen.'

'Why are you doing it, Grace? Such an upheaval, all so sudden, why?' Joel blurted out.

Grace took a quick, sharp breath.

'Surely that's obvious, or do you want it in words of one syllable? I just want to be away from here, start afresh.'

Joel's eyes blazed with sudden anger. For a moment Grace thought he was going to turn and walk out, but with an obvious effort he controlled himself and faced her across the table.

'But you haven't told me why.'

'You mean to say you don't know? After what you did to Honor, let alone Maisie's friend?'

'Maisie? Maisie who? What on earth has she got to do with all this?'

'Oh, nothing. I suppose all that's past history. But you can't ignore Honor.'

'No, of course I can't. And I'm not going to. For God's sake, Grace, what more do you want me to do for her? I can tell you that she's much better and next week she's flying out to Kuwait to be with Ben. She doesn't need me any more, so I can't see what you're getting so worked up about.'

Grace digested this news, resisting the impulse to scream at the man. The calm way in which he delivered it appalled her.

'I see. So you're fobbing her off back to your brother, are you? And what, if anything, does he know about what's been going on in his absence?'

Joel's eyes narrowed.

'What are you getting at, Grace? Why shouldn't Honor go out to Ben? He knows all about the pregnancy. It was a mistake, of course.'

'Of course,' Grace echoed, through gritted teeth.

What an obliging brother this Ben must be, or maybe his moral standards were no higher than Joel's.

'They're getting married, actually,' Joel went on, with every evidence of satisfaction.

Grace repressed the urge to say, 'How convenient.' She felt an overwhelming desire to change the subject. Over the previous days she'd worked hard at coming to terms with the fact of Honor's pregnancy, and she was just beginning to succeed. She didn't want all that mental effort wasted.

'Fine,' she said tersely, 'and now,

shall we have that coffee?'

Joel made a gesture that could have meant anything. Grace poured boiling water into the cafetière and gathered up the biscuits which had scattered over the tabletop. She was intently aware of his dark gaze fastened on her as she poured two coffees and brought them to the table. He looked up at her.

'There's more to it though, isn't there?'

Grace cleared her throat.

'I thought you came round to wish me well for the future. Let's keep it at that, shall we?'

Joel took a long drink of coffee, and she followed suit. But suddenly he slammed his mug down on the table, making her jump.

'It's Simon, isn't it?'

'Simon?'

For a couple of seconds, she looked down at the table top where spilled drops of coffee winked in the light.

'That's none of your business,' she said at last.

'I see.'

Joel's face had a look of complete weariness which cut Grace to the heart. For one brief moment she wanted to go to him, tell him that the hadn't meant any of it, had no intention of getting back with Simon that it didn't matter about Honor, that she loved him, yes, loved him and she would accept him on any terms. But she couldn't bring herself to say if it was too late.

Joel shook his head slowly.

'Well, if that's the case,' he said flatly, 'then there's no more to discuss, is there? I hope you'll be happy up north, Grace, and I wish you joy with your darling Simon.'

'Please go,' she whispered, unable to bear it much longer.

'All right, I will go now.'

He turned and walked away from her through the hallway, but as he opened the front door he paused and fixed her with a long look.

'I just hope you know what you're doing, Grace.'

And with that he was gone.

Grace stood in the kitchen doorway, her body rigid, her hands balled into tight fists at her sides as she listened to the car engine fading away down the street. Then she stumbled into the sitting-room, collapsed in a heap on the sofa and let the tears come unrestrained.

What I've just done, she thought wretchedly, is either the most stupid thing I've ever done, or the wisest. Trouble is I have no idea which.

Grace found to her infinite relief that Joel was not in the department during her remaining few days. He had apparently gone to a nearby university to give a brief course to the medics there. Grace wondered if he'd arranged it at short notice just to avoid seeing her any more. Whatever his reasons, she was glad she wouldn't have to face him again.

Her colleagues took her for a night out and presented her with a crystal vase. Grace was touched at the warmth of her send-off. Several people demanded an address from her as soon as she had one and she received many offers of help with her move. By the end of evening she felt quite emotional.

A lot has happened in the last few months, she thought to herself. I've grown up. I'm my own woman standing on my own two feet. I'm not just an incomplete half of what used to be a couple. If Joel takes the credit for that, then fair enough. At least something positive has come out of all this.

She was aware someone was speaking to her. She turned and found Maisie, Ralph's wife, at her side.

'Maisie, I'm glad to see you! How are you?'

Maisie smiled down a little self-consciously at her growing bump.

'Oh, fine, thanks. Junior is coming along nicely, and I'm past the morning sickness phase now, thank goodness. The worst part is trying to stop Ralph mollycoddling me.'

Grace laughed.

'I'd make the most of it, if I were you. Once the baby arrives you'll have plenty to do.'

'There's plenty to do now, what with getting the nursery ready and finishing the kitchen. I try to do bits while Ralph is away at work, but he complains if I do too much.'

'I'll come and help next week if you like,' Grace offered. 'I finish here on Saturday, and then I have three weeks before I start my new job. I won't need all that time for house hunting.'

'That would be kind,' Maisie responded gratefully. 'You could paint some walls for me. Ralph has a fit if I go up ladders.'

So the following week saw Grace up a ladder at Ralph's home, rollerpainting the nursery walls a soft shade of peach. She was glad to help. Ralph had been a good friend to her during her time at St Margaret's. She didn't know Maisie that well, because Maisie had given up nursing just before her marriage and had gone to work in an office, but Grace had always found her easy to get on with.

'Will you miss St Margaret's?' Maisie asked during a resting moment in the garden.

'Yes, some aspects of it more than others.'

'And some you'll be quite glad to get away from, I suppose. Ralph told me about Joel Kirkpatrick driving you away.'

Grace started to demur, but paused. Something in the way Maisie uttered that name aroused her interest. Then she remembered how Ralph had said that Maisie had come across Joel when she was nursing at Bart's.

'Of course, you met him years ago,' she said. 'What was he like then?'

To her amazement she saw Maisie blush scarlet.

'He was — he was — oh, Grace! If only I could tell someone about it! I've kept things to myself for so long it's really getting me down.'

Grace laid a comforting hand on her arm.

'Tell me, if you like,' she invited. 'After all, I'm going away, so your secret, whatever it is, will be safe with me.'

Maisie looked down at her hands, tightly clasped round her glass of orange squash.

'You'll think I'm terrible,' she said quietly. 'I mean, even Ralph doesn't know about all this. Husbands and wives shouldn't have secrets from each other, should they? But somehow I could never tell him.'

'So why now?' Grace asked. 'What brought it all to the surface?'

'Well, it's Joel Kirkpatrick,' Maisie said wretchedly. 'When I heard he'd come to St Margaret's, I was really shocked. I never expected to come across him again, and then suddenly Ralph was always talking about him, how autocratic he was, but what a brilliant surgeon. And then at the dance I saw him, for the first time in years,

155

and it brought everything back. That's why I wanted to leave early. Ralph thought I wasn't feeling well and I let him think that.'

'So even after all these years you still didn't want to face him. Did you not think that he might have changed?'

Maisie shook her head.

'It didn't sound like it. With you having all that trouble with him, the way he appears to have got his brother's girlfriend pregnant, well, Ralph's been full of it, saying what a heel the man is and all that sort of thing. I've had to sit and listen to it just about every night.'

Grace bit her lip. She knew from experience that once he got a bee in his bonnet about something Ralph did tend to run on.

'Yes, and he did tell me that a friend of yours had a bad experience with Joel years ago.'

'Well, it wasn't my friend,' Maisie burst out. 'It was me!'

'You?' Grace was startled out of her composure. 'But — '

'Oh, I know you must be shocked. Ralph would be. He's very old-fashioned about this sort of thing. That's why I could never tell him the truth about it, don't you see? Before we were married we both worked in London. He was at St Thomas's and I was at Bart's. My little escapade with Joel got on the medical grapevine and Ralph got to hear about it, but he didn't know that I was the student nurse involved. I'd only just met Ralph and I was getting very fond of him. I thought if he knew what I'd done I'd lose him, so I told him it was a friend of mine.'

'I see.'

Grace was struggling to come to terms with all this.

'It was only a brief fling I had with Joel, and it's been over these ten years or more,' Maisie went on. 'It was never anything serious, but you know how things get magnified when people gossip. Joel came out of it rather badly, and he didn't deserve to. That's what upsets me so much. I didn't do anything to correct the stories that were circulating about him, I was too desperate to keep my name out of it.

'Yes, he broke things off between us, but it was because he saw I was getting out of my depth. At the time I was very upset and people blamed Joel, but looking back on it now I can see he did the only sensible thing. And in fact things worked out better for me. I left nursing and I was much happier with an office job, and in time Ralph and I got married and moved up here.'

Grace sat silent, digesting this information. At last she said, 'but what about the married consultant woman? Ralph told me that she deserted her husband for Joel then he left her.'

'Again, that's not quite true. Her marriage was over long before Joel arrived on the scene. She was older than him, and she'd already had a go at one or two of the better-looking young doctors. Who can blame Joel for taking her up on her offer, but when he saw just what she was, he got out quick. Oh, I'm not trying to whitewash him completely,' Maisie rushed on, evidently noting Grace's sceptical expression. 'It's just that I don't think it's fair for him to have this reputation at St Margaret's. He doesn't deserve it, and I feel it's partly my fault because I kept back the truth from Ralph.'

'You mustn't worry about that,' Grace said. 'Ralph doesn't gossip. I was the only person he told about this Bart's business and that was because he thought I was in danger of getting involved with Joel.'

'And were you?'

'I suppose I was.' Grace said, with an unsteady laugh. 'No chance of it now. But look, I'd better get back and finish off that last bit of wall. I'm sure you'll feel better now you've told someone about all this.'

She picked up the glasses and put them on a tray ready to take inside.

Outwardly she was perfectly calm, for Maisie's sake, but inwardly she was in turmoil. So Joel's reputation was undeserved. If she'd known this earlier, would it have made any difference, Grace wondered. The answer came to her almost immediately. No, it wouldn't, because even if his life at Bart's had been one of monk-like chastity, there was still his affair with Honor Delaney. And that was fact. At least it had helped Maisie, getting all this out into the open. Grace intercepted an anxious glance as she unloaded the tray on to the draining board.

'Do you think I was very foolish?' Maisie asked worriedly.

'No more than any young girl getting herself involved with the wrong man. And it all ended happily. You married Ralph and here you are. Maybe one day you'll see fit to confide in him about this. You'll have to see.'

Maisie looked relieved.

'I hope I will. Perhaps after the baby comes.'

'Yes, and, you know, I was just as misguided, in fact more so. I was engaged to Simon for over two years. At least Joel realised you were wrong for each other earlier than that.'

'I suppose that's something I should be grateful to him for.' Maisie managed a smile. 'I hope you'll find someone else, Grace. You deserve it.'

'Well, I'm in no hurry,' Grace said with an answering smile.

As she left Maisie and went back through to the nursery that smile became rather grim, because she doubted very much whether she'd find anyone to arouse quite the same passionate response as Joel Kirkpatrick. And there was no way she was going to settle for anything less.

Later, she arrived home to a quiet house. As she set about making some supper, and getting ready for work the following day, she couldn't help her mind roving back to her last stormy encounter with Joel, right there in her small kitchen. Suddenly it was all too much. She couldn't let it go without one more effort, surely. Thanks to Maisie's revelations she now knew that Ralph had been completely mistaken about Joel. Could it possibly be that she was mistaken about his relationship with Honor? It seemed incredible that there could be any other interpretation of the facts, but surely she owed it to both of them to make one last attempt to find out the truth. A direct question would settle it one way or the other.

She picked up the phone, her fingers trembling, and asked the operator for a new number.

'Kirkpatrick, J. I hope he's not ex-directory.'

'No, we have it here.'

Grace gripped the phone, her knuckles white. Joel would have every right to refuse to speak to her, but all she wanted was just one chance. At least they would be able to part without acrimony. The phone rang and a curt voice answered.

'Kirkpatrick.'

'Joel, it's me, Grace. Could we talk?'

There was a short silence, then what could have been a laugh.

'Talk? What for?'

Had he been drinking, Grace wondered. She persevered.

'There was something I wanted to sort out.'

She took a deep breath. 'I've finished with Simon.'

There was another silence, then came Joel's voice, harsh and bitter.

'Well, fancy that. And how precisely do you expect me to react?'

'Well — '

'Look, Grace, you made it quite plain to me at our last encounter that you wanted to be left alone to run your own life. Off you go and get on with it. You can't have it both ways.'

The phone clicked, leaving Grace still holding on, staring ahead, her eyes unfocussed. He had sounded as if he couldn't care less that she was leaving, and it cut her to the quick. Well, perhaps that was all she deserved. Now she had to start a new life for herself, and hopefully she wouldn't make such a hash of things this time.

9

The seasons moved on more quickly in the north of Lancashire. Summer merged imperceptibly into early autumn, the days shortening, the leaves gradually acquiring the rich tints of golden bronze and copper. Grace sniffed appreciatively as she walked home from work. In the distance, bonfire smoke was in the air, and there was the slight nip of frost in the gathering dusk. But her thoughts were troubled.

Oh, yes, things had worked out very well. She had managed to sell her house surprisingly quickly and had just bought a neat little end terrace in Penrigg, only minutes' walk away from the hospital, with a handkerchief-sized garden. From the windows at the back there was a clear view of the fells, their heather purple beginning to fade into the soft greys and greens of autumn.

The fells — there lay the problem, because up there, only ten minutes from Penrigg, lay Edenfoot, the Kirkpatrick family farm. And worse still, Stella Kirkpatrick, Joel's sister-in-law, worked part-time as a physio at the hospital. All this Grace had learned since starting her new post.

So really, she thought, ruefully, I've shot myself in the foot. Of all the places to choose to move to, I've chosen this. What chance have I that sooner or later I won't bump into Joel, and then what? Perhaps I ought to apply for a job in New Zealand or something. Would that be far enough? Would anywhere be far enough?

And then as she turned the corner from the main street into her own quiet road her heart lurched as she realised that fate had indeed caught up with her. Joel's car was parked outside her door! Immediately she turned on her heel, but too late.

She heard footsteps behind her, and then a familiar voice called her.

'In a hurry, Grace?'

Grace slowed. No point in trying to run away. She forced her features into a mask of unconcern.

'Joel, what are you doing here? Visiting family?'

Joel fell into step behind her, making no attempt to ask where she was going.

'Yes, but that wasn't my main reason for coming. I had to see you. The last time we spoke, on the phone, remember, I was pretty rude to you. I owe you an apology.'

'Apology accepted. There, that was quick. Now, don't let me hold you up.'

'Grace, we can't leave it there. There's something else. What is it?'

Grace, looked up into his eyes and what she saw there made her want to take him in her arms. She saw real pain there, the pain of rejection. So Joel Kirkpatrick was not the self-contained, uncaring individual that he made out to be. But how to explain? How to make him see that it was his attitude to Honor that stood between them? That was something she could never understand, and never forgive.

She owed it to him to define just what her problem was, even though it was painful to her to spell it out, but she's had to try. She drew a deep breath.

'It's Honor. She's what's between us.'

Joel's brows met in a frown.

'I don't understand, Grace. Honor was never anything to me, I thought you understood that. And she's happy with Ben now, so what's the problem?'

Grace stared bleakly ahead, her newly burgeoning hopes plummeting. So it came back to this, every time. He'd got Honor pregnant, but it meant nothing to him. This uncaring, dismissive attitude was so alien to her. This was why there was no future for her with Joel. She pushed past him and hurried on down the street.

'Forget it, Joel. It doesn't matter.'

'Oh, yes, it does. It matters to me. We have things to sort out. You can't run off in the middle of a conversation.'

'Can't I?'

Grace made to pull away again, but Joel seized her hand and held it. She tugged against his grasp.

'Will you let go of me? People are staring!'

'Are they?'

Joel turned and flashed a look which had the interested audience quickly minding its own business. He smiled down at Grace.

'I think they've found something else to occupy them. Now where were we?'

'I don't know about you, but I was on my way home.'

'Then I'll come with you, if I may. We can talk things over there.'

'No! Leave me alone, can't you?'

The instant Grace felt Joel's grip slacken she wrenched free from his hold. She couldn't think straight, she only knew she had to get away, free herself from that disturbing influence that robbed her of rational thought, back to the sanctuary of her own four walls. She set off down the street at a brisk pace, but to her anguish Joel followed.

'I don't want to interfere, Grace, but I want to get things straight between us. I have the strong impression that there's one fundamental fact about this Honor business that has escaped you.'

Grace turned to him. Was she about to hear something that would make all the difference, that would prove to her she'd been wrong about Joel? But how could it be? There was no room for extenuating circumstances; there was nothing he could say to make things right.

'Joel, I — '

The next minute, Grace was slammed back against the wall with a force that knocked all the breath out of her body. As she clutched at Joel's arm for support there was a sudden, earth-shattering roar and a sheet of flame. People shouted and screamed, there was a deafening crash of falling masonry. It was like the end of the world.

There was a horrible, ghastly silence for a couple of seconds then everything went berserk. Nearby a woman started screaming, setting off other voices in a cacophony of sound, shouting, shrieking, calls for help. Panic-stricken people rushed about aimlessly, getting in each other's way. A car alarm was blaring, but no-one was paying any attention to it as Joel and Grace, moved by a common impulse, rushed round the corner to see what was happening.

The sight was appalling. It looked like the whole front of an old stone warehouse block had collapsed into the street. Upper floors were left hanging crazily in mid air, but the heap of rubble at the foot of the building told its own story.

'What on earth?' Grace began as they ran forward, Joel, in front, elbowing a pathway through the crowd.

'Who knows?' Joel threw over his shoulder. 'Gas explosion, maybe. I've seen one before, but not as bad as this. Watch out!'

They were almost at the building now, and as Joel hauled on Grace's arm to pull her back, a piece of roof slipped free and cascaded to the ground yards in front of them showering them with slate splinters. The knot of onlookers surged away farther down the street.

'Out of the way!'

A policeman was running towards them, trying to enlist help in clearing the area.

'For God's sake, keep clear! That lot could come down any minute!'

He made to usher Grace and Joel away, but Joel held up a hand.

'I'm a doctor, and Grace here's a nurse. What can we do to help? Is there likely to be anyone inside?'

The policeman shrugged.

'Dunno. There shouldn't be anyone in the warehouse this time of night, but there was a shop on the ground floor. Could be someone there.'

Then unexpectedly there was an answer to his question. A distraught woman emerged staggering from the rear of the shattered building, her forehead bleeding, her clothing covered in dust.

'Sunniva!' she screamed. 'Where is Sunniva?'

Joel ran to her and guided her away from the building while the policeman and a couple of volunteers kept the growing crowd of goulish onlookers at bay. Grace helped Joel sit the woman down on a street bench and together they made a quick assessment.

The woman's eyes were bright enough, and apart from a superficial scalp wound she appeared not to be badly hurt. She was articulate, but near hysterical. Grace examined the wound which was bleeding freely, and applied a pad made from a clean, folded handkerchief, while she listened to the woman and tried to soothe her.

'What's your name?' she asked, between the sobs and cries.

'Patel, Mrs Patel. But Sunniva, my daughter!' Mrs Patel's face was contorted with anguish. 'She is in there, somewhere. You must find her.'

Joel kept hold of Mrs Patel's wrist where he had been checking her pulse.

'We will, don't worry. But is there anyone else in the shop?'

Mrs Patel shook her head, crying soundlessly. Grace slipped off her jacket and put it round the older woman's shoulders as Joel went over to the fire crew to tell them about Sunniva. She felt desperately sorry for Mrs Patel. The heap of rubble at the base of the ruined building was so big that she couldn't imagine how there could be anyone alive inside. It was a mercy that there had been no-one else in the little shop, but that was no consolation for the poor mother.

'Where were you when it happened?' she asked softly, keeping a reassuring clasp on the woman's arm.

Mrs Patel looked blankly at her for a minute, then she said, 'I was in the store room at the back. I went to make a cup of tea. Oh, why didn't I send Sunniva? Why? Then she would be safe.

She's dead, isn't she? You don't need to tell me, I know!'

Grace shook her head.

'Don't give up hope.'

But Joel's face as he returned was grim, although he made an obvious effort to sound positive for Mrs Patel's sake.

'Apparently the building is very unstable,' he told Grace in an undertone. 'They say the roof could go at any minute. It doesn't look good.'

'But we — ' A siren scream made Grace break off. 'Oh, thank goodness, here's the casualty team. Now, Mrs. Patel, this ambulance will take you to hospital.'

'But Sunniva, I can't leave her.'

Joel interposed, quietly authoritative.

'Don't worry about Sunniva. The fire team will do all it can to get her out. The best thing you can do for her is get over to the hospital and get that head seen to. You don't want to scare her, do you? She'll be taken over there as soon as they get her out.'

175

As the ambulance was driving away there was a sudden shout from the rubble. A fireman emerged waving his arms.

'Quick! Over here! I think we've got something!'

Grace's impulse was to run forward, hoping against hope that they had found Sunniva, but she made herself stay back. It was the job of the emergency teams to cope with the situation, she would only be in the way. She stayed on the bench, watching the group of people near the building as they held a hurried consultation.

'Looks like someone's going in.'

Joel had eased himself down beside her, his eyes fixed on the scene.

'Hope they find the poor kid.'

'Oh, yes! The poor mother, she must be out of her mind with worry. I wish there was something I could do. I feel so helpless here.'

Joel's hand reached out and covered hers.

'So do I. Wasn't exactly the plan I

had in mind for the evening.'

'Oh, that.'

Grace leaned her head back against the hard wood of the bench and stared up at the sky. Suddenly all her earlier preoccupations and concerns seemed so unimportant, especially when compared to a child's life. But, wanting to distract herself from pointless worry, she turned to Joel.

'You never did explain why you were here in Penrigg. Not simply to see me, surely?'

Joel looked rueful.

'Not entirely. But you will be seeing more of me whether you like it or not. I'm going to be working up here. There was a consultant's job going and I've got it.'

'What? But Penrigg is only a small hospital. It's not half the size of St Margaret's. What on earth would you be doing here?'

'I'd only be here one day a week. Most of the time I'd be at Lancaster. I love this part of the world, Grace, so this job was just made for me. But, OK, there was another reason. I wanted to see you again. I thought I could manage without you, but I can't. There you are. Hardly the ideal time or place, but I've admitted it. So what do you say?'

Grace's hands were suddenly damp. He was saying what she so much wanted to hear, had wanted for so long. But had he changed? Had anything changed? Or was she simply being swept along by the emotion of the moment? She turned to face him.

'There was something you were going to say back there, before the building went up, about Honor.'

She waited, breathless, not knowing what she was going to hear and steeling herself to expect the worst. Joel studied her for a while in silence, then he smiled.

'Oh, yes, Honor. This is hardly an ideal time for explanations, but I suppose it's as good as any. I wish I'd realised before that you didn't know the full truth about all that,' he said

178

softly. 'What you thought about Honor and me, I mean. It would have saved a lot of trouble. Honor's baby wasn't mine.'

He paused at Grace's quick intake of breath, then went on.

'It was Ben's. It was all desperately unlucky. He came home for a snatched weekend, without telling his company. He wasn't due any leave, which was why Honor daren't mention it, in case he got into trouble. When, as a result, she found herself pregnant, at first she didn't dare phone to tell him. She only confided in me. I rather assumed she'd told you, but it seems she hadn't.'

Grace didn't dare meet his eyes. Her heart was pounding like a wild thing, and she couldn't trust herself to speak. Instinctively she knew that Joel was speaking the truth — a truth that if only she stopped to ask him directly she could have found out ages since. A flood tide of relief was welling up within her, mixed with deep self-reproach that she'd allowed herself to live with this misconception for so long and failed to trust in him. Why, she could have permanently blighted their chances of happiness.

'Hey, Grace! It is Grace, isn't it?'

A tall woman had come pounding up to them, dressed in the green of a paramedic.

'Could you help us? We've found the girl, but we can't get to her. No one's small enough to get through, but you could manage. Would you be willing to try?'

Three pairs of eyes swivelled to the damaged building. Joel made a low sound deep in his throat and Grace knew he was aware of the danger, as she was herself, but she tried not to think of it.

'Fine, I'll try. Tell me what you want me to do.'

Followed by Joel, she accompanied the paramedic to the front of the building where firemen were busy putting up jacks. An officer came forward and after a hurried consultation with the casualty team he spoke to Grace.

'We've stabilised it as much as we can. The girl's in here, not far from the front, thank God. Can you crawl through and see how she is? We're not getting much response from her.'

Grace glanced round at the worried faces and knew that the situation was serious for poor Sunniva. She took the small torch that was handed to her.

'OK, I'll try. Do I go in here?'

The opening looked ludicrously small, and as Grace bent down and started to squirm inside she had to choke back an overwhelming feeling of claustrophobia. It was surprisingly hot as she inched her way forward, wrinkling up her nose at the acrid plaster dust, grimacing as her arm grazed on a sharp surface, and trying desperately not to cause any disruption of the poised heap. As she disappeared from view she heard a voice behind her.

'That bloody gable end doesn't look

too safe,' followed by a smothered curse from Joel. Hardly the most reassuring of send-offs, she thought grimly.

Gritting her teeth, Grace inched forward. The thought of Joel, only feet away, was a reassuring one. The warmth of his concern kept her going. She shone the torch ahead of her, trying to make sense of the twisted shapes ahead.

'Sunniva!' she called out gently, afraid of frightening the girl.

Her torch beam was pitifully inadequate in the tangle of wood and masonry, and she hoped she was going the right way. With no sound from Sunniva there was no way of knowing. Another large beam blocked her way. After a moment's hesitation she flattened herself to crawl underneath, emerging into a mercifully wider space, and there was Sunniva.

The beam had saved her life, Grace realised instantly. It had prevented most of the wall above from crashing down on her. But she was ominously still, and only when Grace had called to her three or four times did she open her eyes and manage a faint response.

'Hi, Sunniva, I'm Grace. We'll soon have you out of here.'

Grace inched forward to lie beside the girl, taking her wrist and pursing her lips at the faint pulse. It was slow and sluggish, and Sunniva's skin felt cold and clammy.

'How do you feel?'

Sunniva moaned.

'Hurts,' she whispered.

'Where?'

'Legs, mostly. Something's pressing them down.'

Grace shone the torch along the girl's body, and yes, Sunniva was right, a long wooden thing, possibly the remains of a door, covered her from the lower abdomen downwards. She frowned. It didn't look too good. There might be pelvic damage and possible internal bleeding, but at least Sunniva could feel her legs. Hopefully her spine was undamaged. She spoke to Sunniva again, keeping her tone cheerful.

'Right, I'll have to go out again for a sec. I'll bring you something to stop it hurting, and there are one or two things I'll have to do. I won't be long.'

With a final squeeze of the girl's hand, Grace set about wriggling backwards out of the rubble, gasping for breath as she emerged into the glare of recently set-up lighting. There was a buzz of excitement from the onlookers at the sight of her, and somewhere a flash went off. Joel was crouched near the opening. He took her arm as she struggled to her feet.

'Are you OK?'

She managed a smile for him, sensing that he was probably more worried than she was. At least she knew that Sunniva was alive.

'Yes, I'm fine. I've found Sunniva, but I can't assess her injuries properly. She's conscious and reasonably calm.'

Trying to keep her voice steady she explained briefly what was needed. She took a few lungfuls of fresh air before

184

she started to worm her way back in. As she crawled along she was hampered by the bulky bag of equipment they'd put together. It kept catching on things and she had to disentangle it gently in case anything dislodged with disastrous results. It seemed an age before she was back with Sunniva, and the deterioration in the girl's condition gave her immediate concern.

She slipped the blood pressure cuff over Sunniva's arm and checked the pressure by torch light. It wasn't too good. Next she fitted an elastic strap over the upper arm, pulled it tight and directed the torch light on the inner surface of the arm, looking for a good vein. The best she could find was in the wrist, so she swabbed it clean as best she could and then spoke reassuringly to Sunniva.

'You're doing fine. Can you hear them moving the stuff away? You'll soon be out. Now, just a little prick.'

To her intense relief the needle went smoothly into the vein and she was able to take a sample. Then she taped the tubes for the drip into place. Where to hang the bag? Cautiously she groped about and managed to find something protruding from the top of the small cavity where they lay. It would have to do. Just as she got it secured Joel's voice came to her.

'Grace, they're making progress, but they daren't be too quick. The gable or something is looking dodgy. They asked if you might be able to fit a couple of hydraulic jacks under this beam. How about it?'

Grace laughed as she passed the blood sample underneath the beam.

'I'm a nurse, not an engineer! But I'll try if they tell me what to do. Anything to get out of here quick.'

But it was over three hours before Sunniva was lifted clear. Most of that time Grace was with her, attaching the bag of cross-matched blood they'd got for her, talking quietly to her when she was conscious enough to appreciate it. Joel joined in the conversation, too, tantalisingly close but unable to get under the beam that formed a barrier against the outside world. Several times Grace urged him to go to a safer distance but he would have none of it. The firemen passed through a couple of small jacks which Grace positioned under the beams as best she could, but all the same there were several anxious moments when the final pieces of masonry were lifted clear and Sunniva could be carefully eased on to a stretcher with a cautionary spinal splint in place.

Grace eased her cramped body over the rubble. People spoke to her, but she paid only cursory attention. She had eyes for only one person, Joel. He came forward from where he had been standing, and held out his arms. As the ambulance drove away, Grace stepped wordlessly into his embrace, feeling his arms close round her like a promise of utter security.

'Grace, thank God you're all right. I was proud of you there. I felt so helpless with nothing to do.'

'Oh, you're wrong there. I couldn't have done it without you. Knowing you were there and that you cared about me was what kept me going. I was scared that she might die before we could get her out, and yes, scared that the whole place would come crashing down on us, before I'd had a chance to tell you exactly how I felt.'

She stopped, suddenly very aware of what she was saying, conscious of its importance. Her voice was just a little unsteady as she went on.

'I love you, Joel. I don't know when it started, but I'm certain of it now. I'm only sorry that I was such a fool over this Honor business. I believed in everyone else except you. I feel so terrible about that now. How can I ever repay you?'

She stopped as she felt his hand gently cupping her chin, turning her face towards his so that she was looking directly into his eyes, seeing the love and concern expressed there.

'It doesn't matter any more,' Joel said softly. 'What matters is here and now and in the future. And that future is going to be shared between us. That's all the payment I want.'

THE END

*Other titles in the
Linford Romance Library:*

VISIONS OF THE HEART

Christine Briscomb

When property developer Connor Grant contracted Natalie Jensen to landscape the grounds of his large country house near Ashley in South Australia, she was ecstatic. But then she discovered he was acquiring — and ripping apart — great swathes of the town. Her own mother's house and the hall where the drama group met were two of his targets. Natalie was desperate to stop Connor's plans — but she also had to fight the powerful attraction flowing between them.

DIVIDED LOYALTIES

Phyllis Demaine

When Heather's fiancé, Adrian, is offered a wonderful job in America their future seems rosy. However, Adrian's brother, Carl, a widower, asks for Heather's help with his small, deaf son. Help which, as a speech therapist, Heather is qualified to give. But things become complicated when Carl goes abroad on business and returns with Gisel, to whom his son takes an instant dislike. This puts Heather in the position of having to choose between the boy's happiness and her own.

THE PERFECT GENTLEMAN

Liz Pedersen

When Laura agrees to help Anthony Christopher to deceive his family she has no idea how far the web of intrigue will extend, or how it will alter her life. His family is as unpleasant as he promised, but Laura drives away from his funeral thinking she has escaped their malicious clutches. However, this is not so. James Christopher is determined to discover what was behind his cousin's precipitate marriage. He despises Laura and hates the fact that he is attracted to her.

YESTERDAY'S LOVE

Stella Ross

Jessica's return from Africa to claim her inheritance of 'Simon's Cottage', and take up medicine in her home town, is the signal for her past to catch up with her. She had thought the short affair she'd had with her cousin Kirk twelve years ago a long-forgotten incident. But Kirk's unexpected return to England, on a last-hope mission to save his dying son, sparks off nostalgia. It leads Jessica to rethink her life and where it is leading.